P9-DFV-419

MADE YOU LOOK

MADE YOU LOOK

LOOK

a novel by
Diane Roberts

Delacorte Press

Published by
Delacorte Press
an imprint of
Random House Children's Books
a division of Random House, Inc.
New York

Copyright © 2003 by Diane Roberts
Jacket illustration copyright © 2003 by John Haslam

All rights reserved. No part of this book may be reproduced or transmitted in any
form or by any means, electronic or mechanical, including photocopying, recording, or
by any information storage and retrieval system, without the written permission of the
publisher, except where permitted by law.

The trademark Delacorte Press® is registered in the U.S. Patent and
Trademark Office and in other countries.

Visit us on the Web! www.randomhouse.com/kids
Educators and librarians, for a variety of teaching tools, visit us at
www.randomhouse.com/teachers

Cataloging-in-Publication Data is available from the Library of Congress
ISBN 0-385-72979-0 (trade)—0-385-90119-4 (GLB)

The text of this book is set in 13-point Times Column Book.

Book design by Kenny Holcomb

Printed in the United States of America

May 2003

10 9 8 7 6 5 4 3 2

BVG

With so much love and thanks to my husband, Jim, my sons, David and Gregory, and my daughter, Diane Elizabeth, who traveled with me in a real Camp'otel, creating a lifetime of memories!

To my six grandsons: Freese, John David, James, Christopher, Carter, and Collin, in hopes that they land on a game show someday!

To my editor, Wendy Loggia, who upon our first meeting said, "Send me a story"—and I did.

And to my mother, Jessie Lucille Hoskins, my sister, Carole Findlay, and Golly Popo, for their total belief in me from the beginning.

Special thanks to . . .

the Ridglea Branch of the Fort Worth Public Library and librarians Wynette Schwalm, Ellen Warthoe, and Nell Noonan, who said, "Yes you can."

David Davis, Chris Ford, Tom McDermott, Debra Deur, Janet Fick, Kathryn Lay, Jan Peck, Melissa Russell, B. J. Stone, Deborah Sizemore, Sue Ward, and Cerelle Woods for the listening process every Tuesday (and especially A. M. Jenkins).

So many cyberfriends, especially Connie Mulloy and Linda Powley.

Kenny Holcomb for designing this book.

(And the Pope, of course, LOL).

chapter
one

Mom always says the difference between a trip and a vacation is the quantity of dirty laundry after it's over. A visit to Aunt Kate's house would be considered a trip—never lasts more than two days, only one change of underwear, two max. However, traveling from Texas to California? Definitely a vacation.

Dad had been in Los Angeles all spring. But he wasn't on vacation. His aircraft company sent him out there. One of the reasons Dad was asked to go was because he's a brilliant engineer. And he's a great problem solver, too. At least that's what he tells us. His boss wanted him to work out some wrinkles in the L.A. office. It wasn't that he hadn't missed us, but he'd said a million times how much he liked it on the West Coast.

I was busy researching a school project on my computer when *Directions Man* popped up on my Buddy List.

"Hey, Dad!" I Instant Messaged him. Engineers love reading directions, so it's the perfect name for him. "How's it going?"

"Miss you guys," he IM'd back.

"Same here."

"The Pacific Ocean is awesome, Jason, and the weather is fantastic."

"I want to see for myself," I wrote him. Were there palm trees and movie stars on every corner? Did everyone drive a convertible? I could almost taste the salty ocean air.

"You'd love it, Mania Man," came his answer, flying across my monitor. Everyone knows my screen name. I chose it after the greatest game show of all time, *Masquerade Mania*.

It's the best. All the contestants are kids. Almost everyone in our sixth-grade class watches, especially Freddy and me. Even my parents and my pain-in-the-neck older sister, Jen, like it. It's hilarious.

The master of ceremonies is this beautiful long-haired girl named Jasmine. Dad says she gives the show class. At the beginning of the show, she glides down a winding staircase like melting butter. She's awesome. Her cohost is Desmond O. Now, that guy is cool. He wears this wild suit. The stripes on his pants go up and down and the circles on his jacket go across. He has a bow tie that lights up when he talks. I'm sure he's the creative genius behind the show.

Desmond O teases the contestants in the Hot Box. He wants to confuse them so that they'll give wrong answers to Jasmine's trivia questions. Jasmine asks a question and the first kid to press his buzzer gets to answer. The questions are tough. It takes a real brain-o to think fast enough to get them right. After a contestant answers three questions correctly he gets a chance to Spin to Win. His spin could land him on a prize. It's unbelievable what they give away—portable MP3 players with headphones, DVD home theater systems, video games, skateboards, televisions, great vacations, sometimes even college scholarships. Once I saw this kid win an Xbox and a year's supply of video games and he passed out cold. I bet he was mortified when he came to. But my favorite part is when a contestant lands on a *WHOOPS!* That's when the real fun begins.

If you land on a *WHOOPS!* Desmond O makes you do crazy stunts. Like jumping into a tub of Jell-O, or doing a funny dance while Desmond O plays his kazoo. Sometimes he forces a contestant to run an obstacle course against a ticking clock. That's the most nerve-wracking part of all. You never know what to expect if the clock wins. Buckets of slimy spaghetti could drop from the ceiling! You could be pelted with water balloons. Three *WHOOPS!* and *zap!* You're out of the game. You have to be careful or you could go home empty-handed and covered in chocolate syrup.

"Did you catch last night's show?" I typed. I didn't have to explain. Dad would know exactly what I meant.

" 'Fraid not," he typed back. "I was still at the office."

"It was really cool," I told him, wishing he were here to watch it with me like he used to. "A kid dressed up as a tube of toothpaste won a trip for four to New York City!" His costume was flipped out. He'd even carried a plastic bag filled with dental floss.

As I sat at my computer, I got this fantastic idea. I'm always getting fantastic ideas.

"Since you're so great at working out wrinkles," I IM'd Dad, "why don't you work out a way for us to fly to Los Angeles, too?" I was dying to fly on a plane. And not only that, maybe I'd have a chance to get on *Masquerade Mania*! If that happened, I'd be a real Maniac for sure.

"Sounds good," he IM'd back.

"Ejsy?" I typed so fast I didn't realize my fingers were on the wrong keys.

"What?"

I retyped almost as fast. "When?"

"Soon."

Next thing I knew, Dad was on the phone with Mom, Mom was on the Internet checking out hotel rates, I was jumping around the kitchen, and our family was California bound! Well, not exactly the whole family. My bulldog, Patches, would be checking in to the doggie motel. And Baby Millicent would probably stay at Aunt Kate's house because Mom always says he who travels swiftest does not carry a diaper bag. Millicent is two years old. Her track record in the potty-training department leaves a lot to be desired. But sometimes Mom gets guilt pangs when she thinks one of us is not getting a fair shake. So Millicent might luck out and land on the plane with Jen and me. If that happens, I'm letting Jen take care of her. What else is a big sister good for, anyway?

Freddy would freak when he found out about my good luck. He was at a family reunion this weekend or I would have called him the second I got the news. The Wades moved across the street from us the day we started first grade and we've been best friends ever since. Dad says Freddy is like an entrepreneur. Someone who can organize and manage anything.

When Freddy and I were in fourth grade we wanted new bikes. I got one of my fantastic ideas: a neighborhood newspaper. Freddy agreed it was the perfect answer to our money problems. "We'll print all the neighborhood gossip and make a bunch of money," he'd said, his brown eyes gleaming.

We made a couple of neighbors mad, especially Ms. Snodgrass. When the newspaper came off our printer, somehow *Snodgrass* had turned into *Snotgrass*. And to make matters worse, we ran a small picture of her mowing her lawn in her bikini. Right beside the article was an advertisement for joining the local YMCA to lose "those extra pounds." She was not amused. But the newspaper worked. We earned enough money for BMX bikes! A year later we sold the paper to a couple of kids down the street for a profit. Selling the paper was Freddy's idea. Freddy and I make a great team.

I ran across the street to his house Sunday night when I saw his parents' car in the driveway. My brain had jumped into high gear and I knew he'd help me come up with a plan. A plan for California-bound Jason P. Percy to become a contestant on *Masquerade Mania*!

A zillion ideas spun in my head as I knocked on Freddy's front door.

"Jase," he said, giving me a low five. He was wearing an I'M PROUD TO BE A WADE KID T-shirt. "Haven't had time to change yet," he said with a grimace. "Follow me. My grandma sent us home with her amazing chocolate chip cookies."

I followed him in. "But before we eat I've got some news."

Freddy knew how much his grandma's cookies meant to me, so that shocked him enough. But when I announced my news to him, his mouth flew open wider than a train tunnel. His face turned the color of an avocado. He stood motionless, like he was nailed to the floor. Then, after a couple of minutes, he spoke.

"Wow."

"Wow?" I repeated, poking him in the chest. "Is that all you can say? I'm talking game show here. Fantastic prizes. Maybe an Xbox, movie passes for the rest of my life, a trip to Hawaii…"

Freddy's mouth broke into a grin big enough to swallow a banana sideways.

"Cool." He gave me a low five and a high five, a gesture reserved for only the ultimate occasions.

We both knew that the people who got picked to be on the show dressed up in goofy costumes. That was a must. Goofy costumes attracted the most attention. People did anything to get noticed. Some kids even stood on their heads and sang songs. If Jasmine or Desmond O liked what they saw, they'd put that kid in the Hot Box. Freddy and I had watched every show since it was first aired. We knew the rules.

"We've got major work to do," I said as we sat down at his kitchen table. "Besides reviewing every trivia question in the world, we've got to think of a fantastic costume. Something that will really catch the producer's eye." I grabbed a handful of his grandma's fabulous cookies. It was easier to think on a full stomach.

"No sweat," Freddy said, twirling the lazy Susan. "You always win first place for Most Original at the Halloween carnival. Costumes are your specialty. Remember?" He laughed. "Anyone who has the nerve to wear their sister's tutu and dye their hair bubble-gum pink is a shoo-in for a game show contestant. You were the perfect color-coordinated ballerina."

I shuddered, remembering. "Jen didn't speak to me for three months after that," I said. Jen is sixteen going on ten. "When she did talk, she'd call me Mr. Pinkie. She still does when she's mad at me. Which is most of the time," I added.

"I wish I could do something that would make my sister quit talking to me. But so far nothing's worked," Freddy said. Carey Anne was younger than us. Sometimes she tagged along when we went places, but mostly she liked to read and ride her bike with her friends. She wasn't half as bad as Jen.

We sat there for a few moments, thinking. "Everyone in our class thought you were cool," Freddie said. "You won us a pizza party, didn't you?"

"I'm *not* dyeing my hair pink again, if that's what you're getting at," I told him, giving my blond head a reassuring pat. "Dad would kill me."

Freddy and I agreed that I'd need to study trivia like crazy until the day I left for the airport.

There was only one more thing I needed. "You should have a manager," said Freddy, leaning forward on his elbows. "And I'm just the guy for the job."

chapter two

"Patches! Patches, my man. Over here!" I glanced out my window Wednesday morning. As usual, there was Freddy throwing a ball to Patches and Bruno. As usual, Patches looked completely confused. I sighed. What kind of dog gets *confused* by a ball?

Bruno is Freddy's basset hound. He's low to the ground and droopy-looking, but it was a trick. That dog and his short legs could qualify for the Boston Marathon if they'd let him run it. I watched as Patches tripped on Bruno's ears. "I have *got* to work with that dog more," I muttered, grabbing my backpack and jogging downstairs.

My sack lunch sat on the kitchen counter next to a bottle of Li'l Dino Chewables. I glared at the bottle. This had to stop. I was pretty sure that middle school kids did not associate themselves with products that started with "li'l".

"Don't forget your vitamins," Mom called from the front porch. I knew she was having her morning coffee and reading the newspaper. Time out, she called it. But she didn't fool me for a second. The real reason she was outside on the porch was to make sure I didn't wipe out on my bike.

"Yeah, Jason," said Jen from behind the refrigerator door, where she was probably drinking from the milk carton. "You don't want to stay li'l!" she added, with what sounded like a smothered laugh.

"Whatever," I said, ignoring the vitamins. I stuffed my lunch in my backpack and headed out the door.

Freddy and I had ridden our bikes to school for as long as I could remember. Mrs. Wade didn't seem to worry about Freddy riding to school as much as my mom worried about me. I could feel Mom's eyes on my back as I headed out the driveway. If she could have joined the police force just to direct traffic on school days, she would have gone through the police academy. When I finally got to the fourth grade, she quit following me in the car. Once this kid asked me if she was my bodyguard. It was embarrassing.

"Willie Mays," Freddy said when I pulled my bike up beside him.

"Huh?"

"Willie Mays," he said again.

I looked at him blankly, just like Patches had a few minutes before.

Freddy rapped his knuckles on my forehead. "Jason, if you want to get on the show you've gotta spend every waking moment thinking trivia questions." He raised his voice. "Willie Mays."

"Fantastic baseball player," I said, snapping to attention. "Played for the New York Giants."

"And?" he said, giving the ball one last toss to our dogs.

"And," I said, "he played center field. The team moved to San Francisco the same year the Dodgers moved to Los Angeles."

"Okay," he said as we started pedaling. "Three Stooges. Names?"

For a moment I was stumped. I couldn't believe it. We both loved old movies. We even had a collection of them between us. We rounded Clover Lane and coasted into the school's parking lot, where Janet, the crossing guard with badly permed brown hair, gave us her standard salute. "Curly!" I shouted. "And Moe and Larry," I added hastily.

We liked getting to school early because it gave us a chance to play basketball before class. But today we had planned a trivia cram session. We parked our bikes and headed for the picnic area. I slid down the cement bench at the table and put my backpack on it. Freddy was not far behind.

"Watch it," I said, rubbing my hands across the bench. "Someone spilled something sticky here." He moved to the other side. "We have twenty minutes before class." I opened my notebook. "What should we do first?"

"Details," Freddy said firmly. "We need a list of important details about *Masquerade Mania,* and trivia questions. And we need to remember things the contestants do to attract attention. What kind of costumes stand out the most on TV? Pirates? Big hats? Guys dressed as knights? Witches? Wizards? Clowns? Alien robots? Men in black? There are a million things you could wear. We've seen a lot of weird-looking people." Freddy's eyes grew wide. "You've got to outdo them, Jase. Wear something that's never been seen before."

"Like what?"

"Like I don't know yet. You'll have to research it."

We started a list.

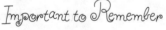

Important to Remember

1. The costume is *crucial*
2. Speak loud
3. Cool props
4. Knowing lots of trivia!!!
5. Persistence

"And don't forget confidence," Freddy added. "That's the most important thing of all. If you act confident, you will be."

He sounded just like our teacher, Ms. Ware. She had lots of confidence. Especially when it came to hairstyles. Sometimes she wore her hair piled into a mountain on her head. She used chopsticks to hold it up. Dad had once told me that Ms. Ware kept honeybees in her hair, and when her students were bad, she'd let them loose in class. I knew he was only joking but I never got too close. Once, one of the chopsticks fell out on the floor and I started hiccuping immediately. I have big problems with hiccups when I'm nervous.

We had seen people on the show beat drums, blow horns, and hold up signs with crazy messages on them. "You need to be outrageous," Freddy said, waving his arms wildly.

I wrote down *Outrageous* and underlined it three times. He was right. I had to wear something that would catch Jasmine's and Desmond O's eyes the second they came into the TV studio—something loud and colorful that would give Mom a headache. Something shiny. Something that made noise when I walked.

Jasmine and Desmond O whizzed up and down the aisles faster than race cars. You had to keep your eye on them or you'd lose track of what was happening. Sometimes Desmond O would shoot a water gun filled with lemonade at a contestant, or throw a cream pie in their face. If they were lucky he'd choose them to sit in the Hot Box. Then they'd get a chance to answer Jasmine's questions. But you had to really watch Des after you landed in the Hot Box because he'd do anything to distract a contestant from answering a question right. If you were sidetracked and missed an answer, a neon sign on his hat would blink MADE YOU LOOK. MADE YOU LOOK. MADE YOU LOOK. Then the audience would crack up laughing because they knew you'd been had. It was great!

"The way I see it," Freddy said, "once you get Des or Jas to notice you, you can talk your way into sitting in the Hot Box. Your big hurdle is going to be answering those questions and ignoring Des and his tricks." He leaned back. "You've gotta be quick with the answers or you'll miss your chance to Spin to Win. You can't hesitate, even for a second, or the other guy in the Hot Box will ace you out."

Freddy was responsible for old movies, history, and music. I had sports, geography, and science. Those categories covered most of the trivia questions they used on the show. We decided we'd both study miscellaneous trivia. I was good with sports, but geography and science were my weak spots. On Sunday we had agreed that Freddy would drill me every day. And he'd kept his promise. Whether I was mowing the lawn for Dad, getting books from my backpack, or running laps in gym, there was Freddy, jabbering away, pitching me one question after another. Freddy would make a great sergeant in the army. He never let up.

"Okay," he said, "let's go over what we've studied so far. When you fly out of here, you're gonna be prepared. I'm going to play Jasmine and shoot questions at you as fast as she does on the show. Ready?"

"Ready," I said, feeling nervous. "Wait," I said as I stood up and pointed to the stairs leading to the front door of our school.

"What now?"

"Aren't you going to float down those stairs and look awesome?"

Freddy frowned. "Would you get serious, Jase? We have lots of work to do, and it doesn't include you trying to become a comedian."

My hands felt clammy and sweat beads popped out on my forehead. Olympian sweat beads. What was it going to be like on national TV if I felt this nervous in front of my best friend? I sucked in my gut and psyched myself up.

"Fire away," I said.

Freddy flipped open his notes. "How many bricks are in the Empire State Building?"

"Ten million," I said.

"What's the dog's name on the Cracker Jack box?"

"Bingo."

"Why were old schoolhouses painted red?"

"It was the least expensive paint."

"Name one of Harry Potter's friends."

"Hermione," I said, wishing I had some of her magic now.

"Which president of the United States owned a parrot?" His eyes narrowed. "And what was the parrot's name?"

"A parrot? They all owned dogs," I said. "No one keeps a parrot in the White House. It's against the law."

Freddy didn't blink. "Who owned a parrot? Okay, I'll even give you the parrot's name. Washington Post."

He was making me nervous. "I'm thinking! I'm thinking!"

"You better think, Jason. You can't hesitate. Not even for a second."

I scratched my head but my brain had fallen out on the ground.

"President William McKinley," he said. "Write it down in your notebook and don't forget it."

I jotted down *William McKinley/parrot/Washington Post.* I looked at my watch. The tardy bell was about to ring. "Time for one more question," I said.

"How many freckles did the puppet Howdy Doody have on his face?"

"Forty-eight," I said, wondering who in the world would ever have counted them. As I slammed my notebook shut, I looked up and saw Amberson Anderson running toward us. Someone had just dropped him off in front of school. He was the only kid I knew who rode to school in a car bigger than the school buses. His folks were loaded and Ambie Boy never let anyone forget it. His freckled face was puffed up from running so hard and I could see his neon braces from a mile away. I wondered how many freckles Amberson had. Just seeing him brought a scowl to my face.

Amberson Anderson was my nemesis. He wanted to do everything Freddy and I did. Ever since his only friend, Paul, had moved away, he followed us everywhere. He was like a second shadow. We couldn't get rid of him.

"Don't breathe a word about this to Ambie Boy," I said under my breath. Amberson was such a big copycat that he'd try to get on the TV show, too.

Freddy's eyes met mine in silent agreement. Amberson bugged Freddy almost as much as he bugged me. He was never without a mouthful of bubble gum, and when he snapped it, it drove Freddy nuts. "You're going to pull out your braces someday," Freddy would tell him. The only reason Freddy tried to warn him was to make him spit out the gum, but it never worked. Amberson would yawn and snap his gum louder. He'd blow huge bubbles and when they popped you could hear the noise all over the school. When a teacher caught him with gum he'd swallow it and say he had already spit it out. I bet his intestines were stuck together with a million pieces of Dubble Bubble.

"Hey, guys," he called, his megabucks sneakers screeching as he stopped. "Why aren't you shooting baskets?"

"We had homework to do," I said, shoving my notebook into my backpack. He looked suspicious. I knew he didn't believe me.

I had to say, it would be funny to see him on the show getting *WHOOPS!*'d big-time. He picked on everyone in class, but I was his main target. Besides copying everything I did, he'd been playing tricks on me since second grade. Ambie Boy did things like leave dead goldfish in my desk. Or spread tacks over the seat of my chair. Once, in fourth grade, he sent a mushy valentine to this girl I liked, Kara Kaye Barton, and signed my name. She totally believed it was from me until he blabbed the truth. I nearly strangled him. I did like her a lot. In fact, I still do. Our whole class thought it was funny. It took our teacher forever to calm everyone down, and Kara Kaye cried. After school I stopped by her house but her mother said she wouldn't talk to me. That's been going on for two years now.

I'd been thinking about next year. Seventh grade would be the perfect time to get a girlfriend. Jen even suggested it, and for once, I thought I might take her advice on something. If I got on TV, Kara Kaye might start speaking to me again. I felt my self-confidence swell in my chest. When you've been on TV (and I'm not talking about one of those reality police shows), people treat you differently. I wouldn't be just Jason P. Percy, the seventh grader, I'd be known as

Jason P. Percy, TV star. And the new owner of a year's worth of DVDs! Things were looking up.

Amberson trailed behind Freddy and me into school. He snapped his gum on the way to class. It was so irritating! I could tell Freddy wanted to sock him. As usual, Ambie Boy was determined to find out what Freddy and I had been doing. No way was I going to let him in on our plans. There were some things money couldn't buy.

chapter
three

School was chaotic before summer vacation. No one paid attention and no one ever turned in homework. I was so excited about going to California that I couldn't think of anything but the possibility of getting on TV. We were leaving the day after school ended. It was hard to concentrate on anything else.

I slipped into my desk and grabbed my math book. Math was the first subject of the day. One year the principal decided to let the students vote on what subject they thought would be best to start off the day. The whole school voted recess first and lunch second. So the faculty voted. Math won out. Big surprise!

Ms. Ware was a good sixth-grade teacher. She believed in giving students the freedom to be themselves. "Soar beyond your greatest expectations," she'd say as the first bell rang. Not a day passed that she didn't write one of her famous quotes on the blackboard. *Dream and you shall become. Just do it. Only hungry minds can become educated.* I copied down her quotes in my notebook. It was corny, but the words motivated me. Jen had been in her class a bunch of years before me. I had always held Ms. Ware responsible for giving Jen false hope about becoming a famous ballerina.

"Before we begin I want to tell you about something special," Ms. Ware said. "After lunch I want each of you to create something that represents a topic you've enjoyed studying at North Hills Elementary. We'll be working in papier-mâché." Everyone cheered. "You may create anything you like." She paused. "Your work must be original. No copycats allowed." When she said that, my eyes darted to Amberson. He stuck out his tongue and scrunched his face. All his freckles ran together and he looked like one big brown blob.

My hand flew up. "Any suggestions?" I asked.

"The choice is yours," she said grandly. "You are the creator of your own art. You may choose to make anything that you have enjoyed learning about while you have been at North Hills this past year—world geography, life sciences, language arts, health and the physical body…"

Some boys snickered in the back of the room. I wondered what I could make. I had enjoyed learning about lots of things, but none of them seemed interesting now.

"After your artwork is complete," she continued, "you'll write a one-page essay about your creation and why you chose it." The class groaned. She took her glasses off and flung her arms toward the ceiling. "I want each of you to soar!" she said. "Anything goes!"

Amberson headed for the pencil sharpener. He didn't fool me for a second. He spent a lot of time in front of our class and I knew the reason why. It gave him a good view of everyone. He could hear and see all. Especially me. He wanted to see what was going on in case he needed to copy somebody's idea. I watched him out of the corner of my eye as I concentrated on my sketch pad and made doodles across the page. I brainstormed ideas of potential *Mania* costumes. If Ms. Ware stopped at my desk she would think I was drawing what I planned to make in papier-mâché.

I had hurriedly finished my math problems and double-checked the answers. I put my paper at the top of my desk. When everyone was finished we always passed our papers to the person on our right for them to check. Some kids were still working. It gave me time to continue sketching costumes. I drew a scaly monster, a vampire, a king with a jeweled crown, a scarecrow, a cowboy, a ghost—there was no end to what I could wear. The only problem was it had all been done before.

After math ended, we went to the media center and

then back to the classroom for language arts. When I sat down at my desk I saw a note taped to it. *What is a PC screen also known as?*

I wrote *Monitor!* and threw the paper at Freddy. He gave me a thumbs-up.

When the lunch bell rang I shoved my papers in my backpack and got in line. "Have anything good?" Freddy asked as we headed to the lunchroom.

"No way," I said. "We ate fish last night for dinner and that's not an option to feed your kid the next day for lunch. Parents have been arrested for less than that."

Martha Stewart would burst into tears if she ever came to our house. My mom hates cooking. In fact, once our oven was broken for six months before she realized it. Here's what happened. She couldn't find her favorite casserole dish one night and after looking everywhere, Dad suggested the oven. There it was, filled with moldy green mashed potatoes. They were hard as cement. She had forgotten all about them since Thanksgiving—which had been six months earlier! Luckily Mom couldn't do too much damage to a sandwich, so lunch was usually safe.

"Do you think Amberson heard us this morning?" I asked Freddy as we walked into the cafeteria. "He's been spending a lot of time up at the pencil sharpener."

The smell of nachos filled the room. Nachos were

about the only thing the school served that I liked. I opened my sack lunch, took out my sandwich, and flipped the lid off my yogurt.

Freddy was already into his dessert when Amberson plopped down at our table with his lunch tray. "Hey, guys," he said, like he was doing us a favor. "I'll eat with you today." Freddy rolled his eyes.

Amberson crammed a handful of nachos into his mouth and the melted cheese dripped down his shirt. He had shoved his plastic cup of jalapeño peppers off to the side of his tray.

"Gross!" I said. "Can't you eat those things one at a time?"

Across the cafeteria, someone dropped a tray. Freddy and I looked up to see what had happened. When I turned back around, Amberson had a smirk on his face.

"What are you smiling at, Cheese Face?" I said as I took a big spoonful of yogurt. "Blechhh!" Yogurt splattered across the table, hitting May Ling in the face.

"Ewwww!" she screamed. Everyone in the lunchroom looked up.

I couldn't quit coughing. Yogurt ran out my nose and down my chin.

"Real funny," Freddy said to Amberson, shoving a bottle of water at me. "What's in that stuff? What did you do?" Amberson didn't crack a smile.

"Just a bit of jalapeño juice," he said, like Freddy had asked him for the recipe.

"Jalapeños! You creep!" I managed to say after a few gulps of water. My throat was on fire!

"Don't worry, Jason, it's nontoxic. A little pepper juice never hurt anybody." He laughed and turned to May Ling. "Sorry," he said. "Jason shouldn't spit food at the table."

Before I could smash Amberson's face to pieces Freddy caught my hand.

"Don't do it, Jase," he said. "You'll get sent to the office. No fighting in school. Number-one rule. Remember?" I clenched my fist and put my arm behind me. Freddy was right. I didn't want to spend any time in detention.

The teacher on lunch duty had walked out into the hall. Of course. Whenever a kid does something mean, the teacher misses the whole thing. I picked up my soggy sack and pitched it into the garbage. There was a stack of paper napkins on our table. I wiped the mess off my face and stormed out of the lunchroom. Freddy ran after me. I could hear May Ling still ranting.

I rinsed my mouth out in the water fountain but the bad taste of Amberson didn't go away.

chapter
four

"Dad!" I yelled when I saw his face in the crowd of passengers. "Over here!" I waved my hands like a football referee and jumped up and down. He waved back. I could tell by his smile that he was happy to be home. "Hey," I said when he got up close. His skin was the color of a walnut. "The California sun must agree with you."

Millicent clapped. "Daddy. Daddy. Bye-bye. Bye-bye."

"California is great, Jason. You're going to love it." He kissed Mom and Millicent and gave me a bear hug. "How's my little ballerina?" he asked, looking around the airport. I hoped he wasn't referring to me.

Mom pointed to the newsstand across the corridor.

Jen looked up, waved, and turned back to her magazine. She was such a brat. She never mentioned Dad unless she wanted an advance on her allowance. But Mom and I were excited that he had come back to Texas to fly with us to California.

"How was your flight?" I asked, straining my neck to peer down the motorized ramp that led to the plane.

Freddy had flown zillions of times. His dad was a commercial airline pilot and his family got free airline passes whenever they wanted them. Mr. Wade had arranged for me to fly with them a couple times, but it seemed every time they got passes for me I couldn't go.

I was pretty sure I was the only one in my class who hadn't flown. I didn't mind Freddy knowing my secret, but if Amberson ever found it out he'd never let me forget it. Not only had he made sure we knew he'd flown all over the world, his family had their own jet! I shoved those thoughts out of my mind. My life was about to change for the better and I couldn't wait. I was finally going to get to do something that Amberson couldn't copy.

"That trip was long," Dad said, stretching his arms. "The legroom gets smaller every time I fly."

Mom and Millicent walked to the magazine stand to get Jen while Dad and I headed to the baggage-claim area. I pretended I'd just gotten off of the plane, too. My heart raced. It wouldn't be too many days before I'd be airborne. I tried to ask interesting airplane questions. "How long does it take to fly to California? Can you see the mountains from the air? What states will we fly over?"

Dad looked startled. "Jason, my boy." When he called me his boy something weird was going on. "I guess your mother didn't tell you." I gave him a funny look. "There's been a slight change of plans," he said as we reached the luggage carousel.

"How slight?" I asked, feeling my chances of getting on the game show going down the tube. The conveyor belt began to move and suitcases spilled out of the chute.

"Mom and I have decided not to fly out to California after all."

"Wh-wh-what?" I stammered. The pizza I had eaten for dinner was about to land in his face. "I thought that's why you came home. To take us back to California!"

Dad reached for his suitcase and dropped his next bombshell. "That *is* why I came home," he said. "We are going to California. But we're not going to fly. We're going to camp."

"Camp?" I repeated weakly.

"All five of us," Dad went on. My knees turned to water. "Camping will give you kids a chance to see the country. It will be an unforgettable experience."

Unforgettable? Camping to California with my parents, Jen, and the two-year-old disposable-diaper queen of the world would be more than unforgettable. It would be disastrous. I panicked.

"But Dad, I'll look out the plane's window the entire time. I promise! I'll see as much of the country as I can. I won't miss an inch of it." Mom, Jen, and Millicent came into the baggage-claim area. Dad gave Jen a hug. She still had her nose buried in her dance magazine. She went over to a bench and plopped down.

I looked at Mom. "Tell me he's joking," I pleaded. "You aren't considering camping to California, are you?"

Mom smiled, putting her arm around me. "Jason, it's going to be great," she said. "I wanted to take a camping trip like this when I was your age, but I never got the opportunity."

"Then why give it to me?" I said.

She laughed. "You'll get a chance to see other states up close. You couldn't do that from a plane window. We'll be traveling across New Mexico, Arizona, and the great California Mojave desert. You'll see parts of the country you've never seen before."

"I know what our country looks like, Mom, I have schoolbooks, remember? This isn't a geography lesson. It's a vacation."

I turned back to Dad. "You can't be serious," I said, tugging on his sleeve. "How can we camp to California?" I brightened. "We don't own a camper."

"We do now," Dad said, puffing up like a peacock. "I

bought Aunt Kate and Uncle Dan's 'miracle of miracles.' We are now the proud owners of the famous Camp'otel."

I felt like I'd landed on a *WHOOPS!* It was the worst possible news he could have given me. Freddy was never going to believe this.

"Sure, we'll be roughing it a bit, but camping will give us the opportunity to get in touch with Mother Nature," Dad said. "Just like the pioneers."

"But Dad," I argued. "Have you forgotten Uncle Dan's horror stories? Mother Nature doesn't want to be in touch. Have you forgotten what Aunt Kate said when they got home? She wished they had taken an ark instead of a camper because it rained a million buckets of water."

"Aw, Jason, what's a little pitter-patter?" Dad ruffled my hair. "We'll benefit from their mistakes. Uncle Dan has already given me a few pointers on what not to do. And I've been reading *The Camper's Friend* magazine." He raised his hand to give me a high five. He slapped my hand so hard that he knocked me onto the luggage carousel.

I was moving along the conveyor belt with the unclaimed luggage when this crazy idea hit me. I'm always getting crazy ideas when I need to solve a problem. And this was a huge problem. Maybe no one would notice me and I could stow away on a plane heading out west. It would take my family at least three days to drive to California from Texas, and I could hang out on Sunset Boulevard until they got there.

No such luck. I felt Dad's hand on my neck as he dragged me off my perfect escape route.

"Dad," I begged again. "Can't we fly?" He held on to my sleeve as he scanned the conveyor belt for his remaining bags. My family didn't know the first thing about camping. We didn't even go on picnics.

Jen still sat on the bench. "Jen!" I hollered. "You don't want to camp to California, do you?" When she realized she couldn't use her blow-dryer in the camper because we wouldn't have electricity, she'd freak.

Mom was busy buckling Millicent into her stroller. Jen peered over the top of her magazine. "As long as I get to shop on Rodeo Drive, stroll down Santa Monica Boulevard, and see movie stars' homes, I don't care how we get there."

Dad smiled and picked up his luggage. "That's the spirit," he said, giving Jen a thumbs-up. My parents started walking through the airport. I ran after them, pushing Millicent in her stroller.

"Wait!" I yelled. I pushed the stroller between two little old ladies at a high rate of speed, knocking one of their purses to the floor. "Sorry," I said, stopping long enough to pitch it to them. Millicent giggled. "Don't you guys ever watch commercials?" My parents continued walking. "Kids twelve and under eat free at the Holiday Inn," I cried desperately. "Doesn't that count for anything?" I ran faster. "A nice air-conditioned motel room with a king-size bed and a color TV.

Room service. Privacy!" Everyone in the airport looked at me as my voice climbed five octaves. I felt a case of the hiccups coming on. "Not the Camp'otel," I pleaded as we went through the wide revolving door. I ran after them to our SUV.

"Waster," Millicent cried, the wind blowing her hair back. "Waster." She clapped her hands.

"You're such a twerp," Jen said when I reached them. "Who needs air-conditioning when they're going to get to stroll down Rodeo Drive? Who needs room service when they might get discovered on Hollywood and Vine?" She tossed her long brown hair to one side. Jen thought three years of playing Clara in *The Nutcracker* gave her the license to act like a prima ballerina. She opened the door and started to climb into the shady side of the car.

"Wait a minute," I said. "It's *your* turn to put Millicent in her car seat." I handed Millicent over and got in on the other side. I leaned against the window. "Who needs a sixteen-year-old sister?" I said out loud, but no one paid attention to me. I was doomed and we hadn't even left town. The Camp'otel was a joke. An overgrown sardine tin perched on top of a car. I'd be the laughingstock of North Hills Elementary.

"Car trips are boring," I said with a scowl. "Boring. Boring. Boring."

Mom turned around in the front seat while Dad put

his bags in the back. "How can you say that, Jason? We're going to play games, sing songs, talk, and be a real family for a change. Dad's really looking forward to this trip. He wants to spend some quality time with us." I grimaced. "He thinks a camping trip will be just the thing," Mom pressed on. "If we flew he wouldn't have much time to visit with us before he's back at work."

"They don't let you talk on airplanes?" I said. She ignored me.

"He wants to know what you've been up to since he's been gone. I need for you to give him a chance to make this work." I just stared at her. "End of sermon," she said as Dad slid behind the wheel.

How was I going to tell Freddy? My pizza wouldn't be still any longer. My stomach gave a huge rumble.

"Mom," Jen shrieked. "Mr. Pinkie is barfing!"

chapter
five

"Let's shoot some hoops," I said to Freddie. "I need to work off some steam." We had time for a short game in our driveway before *Masquerade Mania* came on. I'd been too embarrassed to tell Freddy about the Camp'otel yet, but I knew I was going to have to do it. I pitched the ball to him but it went way over his head. He had to chase it across the street.

"Sorry." I took a breath. Between the art project and Amberson and the camping trip it was hard to focus. Freddy tossed the ball back to me. I started dribbling in circles but I was too preoccupied to shoot. "Let's take a break." I sat down in the driveway.

"What's going on?" Freddy said. "You seem off in space."

I immediately got the hiccups.

"What's with the hiccuping?" he said.

"There's been a switch in plans about our trip."

"What? Aren't you going to California?"

"Yeah, we're going to California all right, but my dad's changed how we're getting there." I shrugged, trying to look casual. "No biggie."

"So? How are you going?" he said. "By covered wagon?"

My hiccups grew louder. "You might say so. Dad bought Uncle Dan's camper."

"What?" he yelled. "That thing your aunt and uncle almost got killed in last summer?"

"You got it."

"That thing that looks like a giant sardine tin?"

"I tried to tell my parents that, but no one will pay any attention to me." I couldn't look at Freddy's face. I was too embarrassed.

Freddy let out a war whoop and collapsed to the ground laughing. He rolled around until I felt dizzy. Tears ran down his face like a waterfall. I had never seen him so hysterical.

"You're kidding," he said when he finally stopped laughing. "I didn't know your dad hated your family."

"You have to swear in blood you won't tell anyone," I

begged. "If Amberson ever finds out he'll never let me forget it. On second thought," I said, "this is probably the one thing he wouldn't ever want to copy."

About that time, Mom came to the door and said our show was starting. "Come on," I said. "Let's go." I looked across the street as we headed into the house. I thought I saw a shadow lurking behind a tree. It was probably just a stray cat, but I wouldn't have put it past Amberson to spy on us even there.

Jen was already curled up on our den sofa eating popcorn and Mom and Millicent were sitting in a recliner across the room. Dad was in his favorite TV chair. I grabbed sodas for Freddy and me and filled up a bowl with popcorn. We plopped down on the floor. The theme song began, Jasmine floated down the stairs, and the show was off and running.

"Look at that guy," I said as Desmond raced across the stage riding a unicycle and juggling balls. "You never know what's he's going to do. He's fantastic."

The camera scanned the audience and focused on this kid dressed like a pig. He held up a sign that said OINK, OINK, I'M A PIG. GIVE ME A CHANCE AND I'LL DANCE A JIG. Desmond O whizzed past him. The kid didn't get chosen to sit in the Hot Box but he made one terrific-looking porker. I punched Freddy in the arm. "He looks great. I wonder why Des didn't pick him for the Hot Box."

"He probably had to get back to the campground so they could roast him for dinner," Freddy said, laughing. I punched him in the arm again.

Mom chimed in. "He wasn't original enough. We see pigs on this show all the time."

"Yeah," Freddy said. "Pigs are out. We've got to think of something better than a pig for Jason."

Baby Millicent clapped her hands. "Oink, oink," she said. "See the pig. Oink, oink." I laughed. I didn't want to be a pig, anyway. I could come up with a costume better than that.

A girl in a straw hat stood up and sang "Hound Dog," and Desmond O rushed to her side. The audience stomped their feet to the music.

"Have a guitar?" Des asked her, grabbing her hat and sailing it into the audience. A million hands reached up to grab it.

"I bet she has one," I said, and before anyone could doubt me, she opened her purse and held up a toy guitar. "That girl is gonna win some money," I told everyone. "Watch."

"I'll give you five hundred dollars for your guitar if you'll quit singing," Des said. Wow. I couldn't believe my ears.

"Did you see that? She got five hundred dollars for a stupid toy guitar!" The girl shut up and sat down. I made a mental note to take a toy instrument along. If I could get five hundred dollars for a toy instrument I'd be happy.

"Where is that pig? Where is that pig?" Desmond O sang out at the top of his lungs. His bow tie twinkled as he ran up and down the aisles. He grabbed the pig's snout and pulled him into the Hot Box.

"Hey," Jen said. "That pig's getting to sit in the Hot Box after all." We all cheered for the pig.

Desmond shoved a boy dressed like a moose into the other box.

"This must be the night for animals," Dad said. He held up his hand and motioned for us to be quiet. "Jasmine is getting ready for her first question."

I edged closer to the TV. I didn't want to miss anything. My notebook was on the floor next to me in case I needed to take notes.

"What was the most important consumer product of the twentieth century?" Jasmine said.

Before they could answer, Mom screamed out, "Queen-size panty hose!" Everyone cracked up. My mom was a laugh a minute.

The pig pushed his buzzer first. "Computers!" he oinked.

"Right," Jasmine said. "One point for the pig."

"Here comes another question," I said, "everyone cool it."

Jasmine smiled into the cameras. "What is the only

letter in the alphabet that does not appear in the name of any U.S. state?"

"*Q!*" Freddy and I yelled together.

"What are those guys waiting for?" I hollered. "Ring the buzzers. Ring the buzzers!" I slapped my hand on the floor. "Uh-oh, here comes Desmond," I said. "Looks like trouble."

"Watch out!" Jen yelled out to the pig. "You're going to get it!" But she was too late. I was laughing so hard it was hard to hear Jasmine repeat the question. Just as Desmond reached the pig, he threw a cream pie in his face. He started after the moose but the moose rang his buzzer.

"*Q!*"

"Right," Jasmine said. "A point for the moose."

"What is the capital of Texas?" Jasmine asked.

We all screamed, "Austin!" The pig managed to push his buzzer first, and he got the answer right, too.

Jasmine never ran out of questions. She spoke into the mike again. "What was the pig's name in *Charlotte's Web*?"

"Unfair advantage," Freddy said, shaking his finger at the TV.

Before the pig could answer, the moose pushed his buzzer. "Samuel."

I put my head in my hands. "What a dork!"

"It's easy being an armchair contestant," Dad said. "Being on the real show is a lot different."

I shrugged. He was probably right, but I knew I'd have known that one.

"Wilbur!" the pig yelled out.

"You get to Spin to Win!" Jasmine said. I sat there holding my breath. When the pig spun the wheel he landed on a BMX bike and five video games. We all sat there not knowing what to expect next.

"Here comes Desmond O," Jen said. "He's after the moose." We didn't take our eyes off the TV. Even though the moose didn't get a chance to spin, his dumb answers got him a *WHOOPS!* Desmond pelted him with water balloons and the moose doubled over laughing as he ran out of the Hot Box. Win or lose, it was the best show on TV. I just *had* to get on *Masquerade Mania.*

After Freddy went home and it was time for bed, I checked over my costume sketches. Then I got one of my fantastic ideas. I raced across the room to my bookcase and grabbed my books on dinosaurs. As many times as I'd seen *Mania,* I couldn't remember seeing a dinosaur on the program. It was perfect!

I had forgotten how much I liked studying them. I'd seen *Jurassic Park* five times and each time I'd been scared to sleep alone in my room for weeks afterward. But now that I was older, I wasn't afraid anymore. Back then, I'd slept by my parents' door. Every morning Jen would come out in the hall and pretend to be afraid. "Mom," she'd fake shriek. "There's a stegosaurus in the hall asleep under his blankie!" She was such a pest.

Molding a dinosaur head in papier-mâché couldn't be that hard. I flipped through the books. Triceratops was cool, but the horns would be hard to keep in place. Stegosaurus was big and ugly. His claws were long and frightening. I wasn't sure how I'd make them. Everyone knew Tyrannosaurus rex—I needed something more unique. When I turned the page to allosaurus, I grinned. I'd always liked the allosaurus. His head was enormous and his body was huge. The picture of the allosaurus showed almond-shaped eyes. It made me think of Amberson.

I logged on to my computer and typed "Entrepreneur" in the address.

```
Hey, Freddy. I've decided what I'm go-
ing to make in art class for a cos-
tume. An allosaurus. See you tomorrow.
Mania Man.
```

chapter
six

"I'll make the eyes big enough to see out of and the mouth large enough so people can hear me talk," I explained as Freddy and I biked to school. "And long, sharp, jagged teeth."

"Totally perfect," Freddy said for the fifth time. He'd decided he was going to make a volcano.

"I'm going to put a bowl of vinegar and baking soda inside the volcano. When it bubbles, it'll look like it's erupting," he said.

"Cool." I could hardly wait to get started.

"Class, are we ready to begin?" Ms. Ware said as we filed into our room after lunch. She acted as happy as if she'd eaten her lunch with a roomful of clowns. Our desks were covered with newspaper and there were tubs of papier-mâché at the front of the class. I stepped around them and made my way down the aisle to the back of the room.

I looked at May Ling when I got to my desk. "Sorry about the other day," I said, scooting into my seat. She looked the other way. I didn't blame her. I'd be mad, too. She hadn't reported me, though, because Ms. Ware hadn't handed me a pink slip from the principal's office. Ambie Boy stood at the pencil sharpener. I knew May Ling hadn't reported him, either.

"People," Ms. Ware said. "You'll need to work fast. We don't have many days left before summer vacation." There wasn't a kid in class that didn't know that.

I loved working with papier-mâché. It didn't matter to Ms. Ware how messy we got as long as we created. The more we worked, the better she liked it. Through the entire art class I molded and shaped, barely stopping to catch my breath.

Ms. Ware fluttered about the room, oohing and aahing over everyone's work. "Look," she'd say, holding up one project after the next. "Isn't this beautiful? Oh, my! This one is wonderful." She had a way of making everyone in class feel special. She stopped by Freddy's desk. "Interesting, Freddy." My desk was next. "What do we have here, Jason?"

I hesitated to tell because I didn't want Amberson copying me. But I remembered what Ms. Ware had said about copying. "It's a dinosaur head," I said. She walked around my desk, looking at it from all sides.

"I'm not finished yet," I explained.

"What kind is it?" she asked, examining the jagged teeth with her fingers.

"It's an Ambie-saurus," I said. I heard some snickers from the back of the room. "I mean an allosaurus. One of the meanest meat-eating dinosaurs that ever lived. He ate anyone who got in his way." I glanced at Amberson. He lowered his eyes.

"Fascinating," she said. "You're doing a wonderful job. I certainly would have been terrified to meet up with that fellow."

She moved on. "And what are you working on, Amberson?" I tried to sneak a look. He stood in front of his desk and it was hard for me to see. "It's an airplane," he said. "A Learjet. My dad owns one." He held up the fuselage so everyone could see. I rolled my eyes. He just couldn't resist bragging about how rich his family was.

"Interesting," Ms. Ware said. "Tell us about it."

"Well, everyone knows about air travel and how convenient it is when you want to get somewhere fast." My stomach did a flip.

Ms. Ware looked interested. She stood there with one eyebrow arched and her arms folded. "So you're making an airplane to show us about transportation?"

"Yeah," he said, shooting me a sly smile. "I guess you could say that."

chapter
seven

Mom was hanging up the phone as I went into the kitchen the next morning for breakfast. "Great news! Aunt Kate and Uncle Dan will be here soon with their miracle of miracles, the Camp'otel." My heart sank. Dad would set the Camp'otel up on top of our SUV as soon as Uncle Dan unloaded it on us. "The only reason they call it that is because they weren't killed on their first camping trip. It's a miracle they came back home at all!" I sat down at the table and reached for the cinnamon toast. Dad said he always knew when breakfast was ready. He heard mom scraping the burnt parts into the sink.

"I'll admit," Mom said, "some of their experiences were gruesome." She poured herself another cup of coffee. "However, Aunt Kate will tell you herself that the good outweighed the bad. She's sure we'll have many memorable moments."

"What she failed to tell you was some of them would be life threatening." I took a crunchy bite. "What about the tree that fell on their car during that rainstorm? What about Uncle Dan's snakebite? Have you forgotten the mud slide?"

Mom frowned. "We didn't discuss those things, Jason. That's why Aunt Kate went into therapy—to forget them. She's trying to help our family have a little fun."

"I don't consider putting our lives in danger fun." I reached for the pitcher of juice. "Hey, I think the bacon's burning," I said.

She lowered the fire and turned the Vent-A-Hood on high. The room filled with smoke but she didn't seem concerned. The fire department had been out to our house dozens of times for grease fires. I shook my head. Mom was going to be a real hazard in the woods. No Vent-A-Hood. No firemen. Smokey the Bear was not going to consider her a friend.

"Dad thought you and Jen would like sleeping out under the stars and cooking over an open fire. It's going to be a great experience. You'll make lots of new friends."

"Don't hold your breath," I said. I grabbed the last piece of toast and headed out the back door. Our teachers had an in-service training day and we didn't have to be at school until after lunch, so I'd get a chance to see the camper.

Freddy rode out of his driveway and popped two wheelies before he came to a stop. "Is this the day?" he asked.

"Yes. Aunt Kate just called." I looked up just in time to see Uncle Dan and Aunt Kate pull into our driveway. Uncle Dan blasted the horn. Mom, Jen, and Millicent ran out to see the camper. Aunt Kate waved like a queen on a float in a parade. You couldn't miss the grin on Uncle Dan's face. He looked like he'd made the sale of the century. Even Patches acted excited. Freddy, Jen, and I sat on the ground and watched Uncle Dan and Dad switch the camper from Uncle Dan's old sedan to our SUV.

"Let's open it up so the kids can see," Dad said to Uncle Dan. The system was supported with four legs. Each leg was secured to the rack on top of the car. The camper could be set up in about ten minutes and taken down again in the same amount of time by one person. I had to admit it was clever.

"What about it, kids?" Dad called over to Jen and me. "See?" He gestured proudly. "It's amazing. We have everything we need for a great camping trip." I could tell from the look on Dad's face that he was determined to make a better camper than Uncle Dan had. He held the book of directions Uncle Dan had brought him close to his chest. From what I'd heard about Uncle Dan's camping trip, I figured if he had been a pioneer he would have died the first day on the trail.

Dad would study the booklet thoroughly before we left town. He'd follow all the directions. He'd be prepared.

So would I. I had gone so far as to dig up pictures of Uncle Dan's swollen leg after the snakebite. His cheeks were puffed out like a soufflé and the look of pain on his face was pathetic. I was waiting for the perfect time to show them to everyone as a reminder.

Millicent pounced on my lap. She kept bouncing on my legs. I couldn't imagine what she'd do cooped up in a car for hours at a time.

Mom and Aunt Kate went through all the equipment that came with the Camp'otel.

"Everything's so cute," Jen said, giggling. She had always been a traitor.

The camper was a self-contained system. It not only had bunking accommodations on top of our SUV, but a two-burner Coleman stove, space for two water tanks, two benches that were used in combination with the stove house to make a picnic table, a portable potty, and a ladder for climbing from the ground to the top of the car.

"Check it out," said Freddy admiringly. I glared at him.

One of the water tanks was used for drinking water and the other was used for taking a shower inside a circular curtain that was also stowed in the system. The shower was set up beside the car. It had a flimsy red-and-white plastic curtain that reminded me of an old-fashioned barber pole. Maybe someone would think we gave haircuts and we could earn some money along our way. When Dad set up the shower I started laughing.

"What's so funny, Mr. Pinkie?" Jen asked.

"I was just imagining you showering in front of total strangers in a plastic shower cap. That's all."

"They have nice bathrooms at those campgrounds," she snapped. "We don't have to use this shower unless the bathhouse is full. Mom showed me the brochures. And for your information," she continued, "all the showers have doors. There's plenty of hot water, too! The brochures promised."

Just watching Dad set up the camper was making me feel crabby. "*Duh,* Jen. They camouflage the bad stuff in those brochures so people will be tricked into staying there."

"Like you would know!" she said in a huff. Then she grabbed Millicent's hand and stomped away. Freddy grinned. Sisters.

"Jeez, Jason," Freddy said when the camper was completed. "Too bad P. T. Barnum isn't here. He'd have loved the Camp'otel"

"Huh?" I said. "Who?"

"P. T. Barnum. Don't you remember? 'There's a—' "

Freddy had snuck in another trivia question.

" '—sucker born every minute,' " I finished sadly, looking at Dad and shaking my head.

Aunt Kate kept insisting there wouldn't be much dish washing on our trip. "Use paper for everything."

Aunt Kate was very into paper. When she and Uncle Dan were engaged, Aunt Kate got it in her head that she wanted a throwaway paper wedding dress. Apparently she'd read about some eccentric actress who'd had one. And since it was Aunt Kate's third wedding, I guess she didn't want to be out a lot of money on a dress. If this marriage didn't work, she told Mom, she could always line the bottom of her birdcage with it. No big deal.

"Oh, Kate!" Mom said when she brought the dress by for us to see. "It's lovely." Even I had to admit it wasn't half bad. Aunt Kate had floated down the aisle like a paper princess. Her long white train rustled behind her as she walked toward the altar. It was at the reception that the paper hit the shredder, so to speak. Just as the happy bride and groom were about to make a wedding toast, Uncle Dan, who had drunk one too many glasses of champagne, knocked over two candelabras. Before anyone realized it Aunt Kate's wedding train went up in smoke. Everyone threw their champagne on the fire, and poor Aunt Kate looked like a soggy paper napkin when she left for her honeymoon.

"I hope it doesn't rain when we eat at the campgrounds," I said. "We all know what water does to paper."

Uncle Dan's face turned the color of a tomato. No one said another word about the wonderful Camp'otel.

I lay back in the grass, resting my head on my hands. There were a million clouds in the sky. One of them looked exactly like a dinosaur. Maybe camping wasn't going to be so bad after all. If that was the only way I could get to California, then I guess I'd have to do it.

"Well?" Freddy said.

"Well what?" I said, sitting up abruptly.

"I wonder if your uncle Dan is going to mention his snakebite." Freddy crossed his arms over his chest. "That reminds me. "Who was the founder of the American Red Cross?"

"Clara Barton," I said. "May 21, 1881."

"Name five poisonous snakes."

I shook my head. "You don't let up, do you?"

"A good manager never lets his client rest," he said, punching me in the arm. "Well, come on. Quick."

I held four fingers in his face. "Rattlesnake. Coral snake." I got goose bumps thinking about them. "Cobra. Water moccasin."

"Good answers," he said. "One more."

I held up my thumb. "And Amberson." I laughed. "That makes five."

chapter
eight

I coasted across our yard as Mom pulled into the driveway. Patches ran to greet me like he always did when I got home from school. I threw a ball for him to catch, and without Bruno around he scored big-time.

Mom honked the horn and waved. "Help me carry in these groceries. I did the shopping for our trip." She got out and handed me a couple of sacks. "Why are you so late? I was just about to call the school."

"Ms. Ware is having us soar again," I said. "We're making papier-mâché sculptures and we had to clean up before we left." I looked at my watch. I was only ten minutes later than usual but I knew there was no sense arguing about it.

"What's your project?"

"An allosaurus head. I'm going to use it as my costume when I try out for *Mania*. It's awesome."

"We're taking lots of stuff with us, Jason. Can't you use something else? I don't think we'll have room for an allosaurus head in the car. Especially if it's large."

"We've got to have room, Mom. It's impressive. Wait till you see it," I said. "There's lots of storage space behind the third seat." That's where I was planning on riding during the trip.

Mom shrugged. "Dad will have to see if he can make it fit somewhere in the car, then. You know him. He loves solving a problem."

"I've got a problem I wish he'd solve."

"What?"

"Amberson Anderson! He's a jerk, Mom. He follows me everywhere I go and he's always trying to butt in with Freddy and me. He's a big copycat." I didn't usually tell my mom about my problems at school. Knowing her, she'd have me signed up for workshops like Bullies Are Potential Friends. But for some reason I was feeling talkative.

"When someone copies you it's a form of flattery. He probably wants to be like you," she said. "Maybe he just wants to be friends. Have you ever thought of that?" I should have known she'd say something like that. My mom was a travel agent for guilt trips.

"He sure has a funny way of showing it. He plays mean tricks on everyone, but I'm his main target."

"Tricks? What kind of tricks?"

"Like the dead goldfish in my desk that time."

"That was a couple of years ago. I thought he'd outgrown that sort of thing. He hasn't done it again, has he?"

"No. He was banned from the fish tank. But he never runs out of ideas. Like stealing my homework and putting valentine stickers on it before turning it in to Ms. Ware."

Mom laughed. "She didn't believe *you* did that, did she?" She reached for a sack of groceries and started putting them in the cabinets.

"I don't know. She looked at me funny all day." I stuffed a bag of pretzels into the oven, Mom's extra storage space. "One time he told the school nurse I was barfing and she rushed into class with a wet rag for my face. He does stuff like that all the time."

I didn't mention the jalapeño juice in the yogurt. Mom would rush me to the emergency room and have my stomach pumped. If she only knew about the food coloring in my lemonade the week before or the salt Ambie Boy puts in my milk every chance he gets, she'd have me admitted to Harris Hospital for observation. Any mom who puts thermometers and an economy box of Band-Aids in their kid's Christmas stocking is a little overprotective.

I put the last sack of food on the table. "It looks like you're planning on feeding the whole state." I didn't dare ask who was going to do the cooking. I took a dish of leftover banana pudding from the fridge and sat down at the table. A sour smell filled the kitchen when I pulled the lid off.

"Sick," I said, waving around the stench. Mom turned to see what had happened. "What kind of pudding is green?"

"Don't eat that," she said, as if I was still considering it. She jerked the bowl from my hands and dumped it into the sink.

"Maybe I should take some to school tomorrow and share with Amberson."

"Jason! I wish you wouldn't joke like that."

"Who's joking? He tried to poison me the other day with jalapeño juice in my yogurt." Oops. "Green banana pudding would serve him right."

"You didn't eat it, did you?" she asked, feeling my forehead.

"Mom, I'm okay. I don't have a fever. I don't need to go to the emergency room and I'm not going to die. But that's the sort of thing Amberson does. Do you think offering me yogurt mixed with hot-pepper juice sounds like he's trying to be my friend? Or that sending mushy notes to Kara Kaye and signing my name to them is something a real friend would do? Or telling the basketball coach that I had quit the team when we went out of town over the weekend and I missed the game?"

Mom pursed her lips. "Sounds to me like he's trying to get some attention from you."

"He's got it all right," I said. "I nearly creamed him the other day. I would have, too, if Freddy hadn't stopped me."

Mom sighed. "His parents don't spend a lot of time with him. I saw his grandfather the other day at the bank. He told me Amberson's parents are going to Europe this summer and that he'll be taking care of Amberson. He sounded interested in our camping trip."

"Mom!" I screeched. "How could you? You didn't tell him about the show, did you?"

"No." She winked. "But I'm sure he'd root for you to win." I could feel a good case of hiccups coming on.

Mom smiled. "Sit down, Jason, and stop worrying. I have some good news, some bad news, and some great news."

"Give me the good news first," I said. "It's been a long day." She handed me a piece of chocolate cake. I checked it out before I took a bite. Mold was hard to see on chocolate frosting and I didn't want to take any chances.

"The good news is," she said, pouring me a glass of milk, "we have reservations in the RWU Campgrounds all the way to California."

"That's good news? What are RWU Campgrounds?" I asked warily.

"Relax With Us Campgrounds. They have everything campers could possibly need or want. There are bathhouses, laundry facilities, computer and fax machines, picnic tables, big shade trees, hookups for people who need air-conditioning, running water, lights, and best of all, playgrounds." She unfolded a brochure. "See?" She pointed to grainy pictures of basketball and shuffleboard courts. "Some even have swimming pools." She sat back in her chair and beamed like she had just been selected spokesperson for the RWU Campgrounds of America.

"Gee, can we play Red Rover, too?" She didn't laugh.

I took the brochure and scanned it. At least there would be computer hookups. I'd be able to e-mail Freddy every day.

"Jen and Millicent can play on the swings," I said, tossing the brochure back on the table. "I won't be leaving the backseat until we hit Beverly Hills. I need privacy."

"Privacy isn't one of the features of a camping trip." Then she made another announcement. "No one is sitting behind the third seat. We're using that space for the cooler, blankets, pillows, games, books, and anything else we might want during driving time. One of you will have to crawl over the seat and get us snacks when we make pit stops."

"So what's the bad news?" I asked. I couldn't imagine it being worse than being squished behind Jen and Millicent.

Her face turned pink. Surely she hadn't invited

Amberson on our trip, but you could never tell with Mom. She was a surprise a minute. "We're traveling light. Each of us can take only five changes of clothes, two pairs of pajamas, one robe, one pair of shoes, and a swimsuit. That's it. We can take only what fits into a small duffel bag."

My hiccups had stopped but I started laughing like crazy. "Have you told Jen?" My sister changes her clothes five times a day, six if it's a school day. Mom went on to explain that the Camp'otel wasn't big enough for all of us to sleep inside. Jen and I would be sleeping in a tent next to our car. My laughing stopped. The tent was large enough for four people and we'd have plenty of room, but strangers could walk by our tent at night, going to the bathroom, or the office, or who knows where? There were going to be animals lurking around, too. If we weren't careful we could find ourselves sharing our tent with some strange varmint.

"Oh, great," I said, thinking of Jen. "I could be sleeping with two skunks instead of just one. Jeez, Mom. All of this sounds like bad news to me."

"Jason," Mom said. "It would be much nicer if you'd try to cooperate." I gave her a faint smile and started up the stairs to my room.

"Don't you want the great news?"

I went back into the kitchen. "Yeah. Shoot, Mom. Anything you say will be great news after hearing what you just told me."

"Dad and I know how disappointed you've been about the plane." I waited. "So...since we're sending Jen to ballet camp at the end of the summer we decided you could take Freddy with us to California."

"Really?" I shouted.

Mom nodded. "His parents have already said it's okay. And Freddy's said yes. He's waiting to hear from you."

"Wow!" I yelled, grabbing Mom and swinging her in a circle. "Thanks, Mom. That *is* great news!" Freddy's phone was busy, so I raced upstairs and logged on to my computer. The dark screen sprang to life. I typed in my password. Then I put "Entrepreneur" in the address.

Hey, Entrepreneur! With a manager like you I can't miss getting on the show. Don't forget to watch tonight. You're taking your life in your hands coming with us but there's a sucker born every minute. Right? P. T. Barnum said so. Welcome aboard, sucker. Masquerade Mania, here we come! Mania Man

chapter
nine

I was in the middle of writing my essay for Ms. Ware when Jen's signature four-rap knock jolted me from my desk chair.

"Hey, Jason?" she said through the door. "Can I come in for a minute?"

I waited. Then I frowned. Jen usually stormed right in after her knock. Something was up. "I guess," I allowed graciously, still on a high after Mom's great news. "For one minute."

"I've never seen you work so hard on a project before," she said, eyeing the computer. "This must be something special."

"My class is voting on the best art project and essay. The person who gets the most votes gets free movie tickets every weekend for the whole summer." I laced my fingers behind my head. "I plan on spending my summer at the movies."

"That sounds like something Ms. Ware would do," Jen said. "She's the best." She did some weird dance move across my room and knocked over my desk lamp.

"Hey!" I said. "Watch out."

"Sorry." She picked up the lamp and sat on my bed. The allosaurus was next to her, wrapped in a black garbage bag.

"What's this?" she said, pulling off the garbage bag. To say she jumped into the air wouldn't exactly be telling it correctly. She bounced higher than a kangaroo. "That's ghastly!" she yelled. "Is *that* your art project?"

"Yeah. Isn't it great?"

"Those teeth are gross!"

"Dinosaurs were vicious, Jen. What did you want me to do? Put a big smile on his face?" She covered it up and moved to the other side of my room. I grinned. It was a perfect reaction. I wanted him to scare people.

"Okay, here's the thing. I need a favor," she said, twisting a strand of her long brown hair. "Nothing big, really."

"What sort of favor?" I said suspiciously. Any favor Jen wanted was a big favor.

"I'll do the dishes for one month when we get back

home if you'll help me out with a small problem. I promise." She smiled. Her teeth were almost as scary as the allosaurus's. "I need to put some clothes in your bag."

"What?" I exclaimed.

"There's no way I can go to California with only five outfits." Jen gestured to my closet. "You wear jeans all the time anyway. You'll take two pairs instead of four." She made it sound like a done deal.

"Oh, no," I said, shaking my fist at her. "Where were you when Mom and Dad came up with this crazy idea in the first place? You had your nose stuck in that dance magazine. And where were you when we were watching Dad set up the Camp'otel? Giggling on the lawn and telling Dad how cute the camper looked on top of our car. And"—I slammed my pencil down on my desk—"why didn't you speak up when you learned we could take only a few clothes?" I got up and opened my bedroom door. "Out," I said, pointing into the hall. "No deal. Freddy and I need all the space we can get. There isn't room for any of your stuff in our bags."

Jen opened her mouth.

"Not even one ballet shoe!" I finished before she could speak.

Jen stormed out. "Twerp! Just see if I *ever* do you a favor!"

I sat back at my desk and spun around in the chair.

So Jen needed a favor from me. She didn't know it, but maybe I would make a trade with her—and it wouldn't be for doing dishes.

◌ ◌ ◌

"Check it out!" Freddy said as we walked into class after lunch. There were tables at the front of the class, and our projects were arranged on them, with the name of each student on a small card in front of his project. As far as I could tell, everyone had soared. Bobby Jones had made a fantastic piano keyboard. Trevor Norman had made a map of Europe. He had marked all the famous battles of World War II with toothpicks. Jenna Dodd's Eiffel Tower had an elevator inside it. Wesley Grant had made a perfect replica of the Statue of Liberty. My allosaurus sat next to Freddy's volcano.

We took our seats. I shot a look at Amberson. He was looking expectantly at Ms. Ware. I'd noticed that he hadn't so much as glanced at my project. But he had been in the room when Freddy and I came in. That worried me. I craned my neck to look at the dinosaur head. It looked okay. But then, so did Jen's room, and who knew what lived in there? With a sigh, I settled back in my seat.

Kara Kaye went first. She'd made a funny little man standing on his head. I had wondered about Kara Kaye's creation but I had been so busy that I hadn't asked her about it.

Not that she would have answered me, anyway. She explained that Lewis Carroll was her favorite author and in his poem "Father William," he had written about a man who stood on his head. Freddy was next. He put his bowl of vinegar and soda inside his volcano. Bubbles floated up into the air. The class loved it. The reports went on all afternoon. We only had time for one more before school was out—mine.

I took out my essay and walked over to my allosaurus head. *Stand straight!* My mom's voice echoed through my head. *Use your outside voice!* Amberson sat in the back of the room trying not to pay attention to me, but I knew he was listening. Some of the girls looked afraid. I was glad. I wanted my allosaurus to look scary and real.

I cleared my throat. "The allosaurus. The allosaurus was wild and wicked." I turned and pointed to the head I'd made. Suddenly I felt like a jerk. All dinosaurs were wild and wicked. What a dumb thing to say!

"The allosaurus had razor-like teeth," I continued. Ms. Ware had put the head on a stack of books so everyone could see it better. "It was one of the meanest meat-eating dinosaurs that ever lived. It ate anything that got in its way." I raced through the rest of my dinosaur facts. At home it had taken five minutes but here I finished in about thirty seconds. "My advice is to stay away from an Ambie-saurus—I mean, an allosaurus—if you ever happen to see one," I finished, gulping. "Thank you." Amberson staring at me made me totally nervous. Everyone clapped. I had messed up but my allosaurus was vicious-looking and a couple of girls screamed every time I pointed to it.

"Put on the head," Amberson said before I could sit down. "It looks so real. We want to see what a vicious allosaurus looks like with a body." I hadn't tried on my allosaurus head yet but I knew it would fit. I had taken a million measurements to be sure.

"Put it on!" the kids chanted. "Put it on!"

Ms. Ware quieted the class. "The bell's about to ring, but if you want to model it, go ahead, Jason," she said. "You've done an outstanding job."

Flushed with pride, I put the dinosaur on my head. I could see the class through the razor-sharp teeth. Then, without warning, the top set of teeth fell to the floor. Something gooey ran down my face and the back of my neck. There was a smell of peanut butter and raspberry jelly inside the head. My allosaurus had been sabotaged!

◎◎◎

It took forever to get home. I barely saw the street as I pushed my bike along next to Freddy. People honked their horns and called out stupid things.

"Yo!" one guy yelled. "Run for your lives! There's a dinosaur loose!" He slapped the side of his car and sped away. We didn't pay attention to him.

"Turn left," Freddy said. "Okay, now right." I could see part of the street through the mouth of the allosaurus head. Ms. Ware and a custodian had tried to pry the head off for ten minutes without destroying it. Finally they gave up and Ms. Ware sent me home with a note for my parents. Patches went wild when he saw me. At first he didn't recognize me. Then he sniffed my shoes and his tail started to wag. I didn't know whether he recognized me or smelled the peanut butter. Dad was standing next to the SUV when Freddy led me to the driveway.

"I know this may sound like a crazy question, Jason," Dad said, "but why are you wearing a T. rex head?"

"It's not a Tyrannosaurus rex, Mr. Percy," Freddy said. "It's an allosaurus. This is Jason's project for our last week of school. Don't you think it looks real?"

"Ridiculous is more like it," he said, distracted, as he opened the back door of the SUV and peered inside. "Take it off, Jason. I need you and Freddy to bring me your bags. I want to see how everything is going to fit in our car."

I turned to face him. Some of the peanut butter and jelly had oozed down my nose. "If I can," I said. "The head is stuck to me. I think I'm going to have to wear it to California."

Dad laughed. Apparently he found my situation

amusing. "What do you think the RWU campers would say if I drove up with a dinosaur in my car?"

"Not as much as they'll say when they see our camper," I whispered to Freddy. Dad didn't hear me. Freddy and I worked for ten minutes until the head finally came off in one piece. We didn't want to destroy it. I had to wipe out the inside. It was covered with peanut butter and jelly. We found enough glue in my desk to put the teeth back on.

"Good as new," I said, sitting on the kitchen floor. "But breaking dinosaur teeth may be a reason to go to detention. Can you believe that guy?"

"Forget it," Freddy said. "He's totally going to pay for it—Ms. Ware will see to that. And besides, the head is fixed now. I'm going to go get my stuff. I'll be right back."

I stumbled into the bathroom. There was peanut butter and jelly in my hair, on my eyebrows, up my nose, in my ears, down my chin—everywhere. While I was in the shower I planned how I could get back at Amberson and not get caught. I'd have to wait until after our trip. If I caused him any bodily harm, Dad would leave me at home and I'd never get on the show.

The next day was the last day of school. May Ling read her essay about the Leaning Tower of Pisa. She had seen the real tower in Italy. Hers was totally authentic. It leaned to one side without falling down. No one knew how she did it and she wouldn't tell. When she finished reading, she put the tower on the floor next to Amberson's jet and gave it a little shove as she walked back to her seat. It fell over, spilling gooey red poster paint out the windows. Paint went all over Amberson's plane.

"Hey!" Amberson yelled, running to the front of the room, but it was too late. His jet was splattered. I wanted to clap.

"Oh, sorry," May Ling said, grinning. "I guess my tower wasn't as strong as I thought." I cracked up. Served him right. I wish I'd thought of it. When May Ling walked back to her desk she gave me a high five. I was glad she wasn't mad at me anymore.

Amberson had to stay in the principal's office during our farewell party. Ms. Ware sent cookies and punch to him. Our class voted on the best art project and May Ling won hands down. I was glad for her. Ms. Ware told us how much she had enjoyed having us in her class. She went to the blackboard for the last time and wrote: *If you don't follow your own dreams, you'll follow someone else's.* That made sense to me. I was going to follow my own dream and get on *Masquerade Mania* if it was the last thing I ever did!

chapter
ten

I woke up at the crack of dawn. Normally on the first day of summer vacation I sleep in until lunchtime. *That's* how excited I was. It was still dark outside. I grabbed my video games and ran downstairs. Dad and Mom were finishing their coffee. Dad was wearing his fisherman's hat with the feather on it. Mom had on a fanny pack and bright blue Bermuda shorts. She wore a straw hat bigger than she was. Their nerdiness didn't even faze me. Who cared? We were going to California!

"*Masquerade Mania,* here I come," I said, putting my allosaurus down on the floor.

They both grinned. "We'll be rolling shortly," Dad said. I shoveled cereal into my mouth as fast as I could.

"I'll let you know when it's time to get on the road,"

Dad called out a little while later. He had made a dozen trips to the SUV. Mom was running around after Millicent. Jen hadn't said much. She wasn't really awake yet.

Mom had spent all week getting Millicent's stuff ready. There were diapers and wipes, spoons and sippy cups, bibs and baby wash. Two-year-olds require *a lot* of gear. The most important thing, however, was Lulu. She was Millicent's fuzzy pink elephant. Lulu went everywhere with her. Millicent wouldn't eat unless Lulu sat next to her. She wouldn't sleep unless Lulu was ready for bed. Lulu had a way of disappearing at the worst possible moments. And when she disappeared everything stopped. Houdini could have used Lulu in his magic act. *Poof!* She could vanish in an instant.

I walked through the house to make sure I hadn't forgotten anything. Millicent's harmonica was on the kitchen table. She had received it as a party favor. Freddy and I had been goofing around the other day and I'd learned a few simple songs. I stuffed it in my pocket just in case Jasmine or Desmond O asked for a harmonica concert.

The doggie motel had been booked, but Carey Anne had agreed to keep Patches. Uncle Dan had said he'd play ball with him. "I'll get him in shape," he'd told me. I didn't hope for much. Uncle Dan's only exercise was walking to and from the fridge.

Freddy and I had gone over every imaginable trivia question. I had so much information buzzing in my head it was leaking out my ears. We'd IM each other every night after the show. Freddy would ask questions and I'd have to give the answers immediately. I felt confident and prepared. Freddy wasn't interested in getting on the show—he was happy to just manage. I planned to share whatever I won with him. That seemed like a fair exchange for all the work he had done.

I took my things out to the car. Jen's bag was already there. It was fatter than a hippopotamus. I wondered if she had cheated and brought more than five outfits. It would be just like her to do that.

Freddy and I sat on the front porch while Dad finished checking out all the camping equipment. It was eerie being up so early when everyone in our neighborhood was still asleep. Freddy's parents were talking to Mom in the kitchen. I looked up at the moon. "Funny, isn't it?" I said.

"What?"

"That the moon doesn't really give off any light. It's only a reflection of the sun's light."

"That reminds me," Freddy said. "How does the earth move?"

I groaned. "It revolves around the sun and rotates on its axis."

"Who was the first man to walk on the moon?"

"Neil Armstrong."

"How many planets move around our sun?"

"Gee, don't you ever give up?" I said. "It's too early to think."

"How many?"

"Nine." I looked at him. "I know. I know. Name them."

"I am *such* a good manager!" Freddy shouted.

"Saturn, Mars, Mercury, Venus, Uranus, Neptune, Jupiter, Earth, and..." I was stumped.

"Cartoon character...?" Freddy prompted.

"Pluto!"

Our parents walked out onto the porch. It was time to leave. Freddy's parents gave him a million hugs before he escaped. We crawled into the third seat of our SUV. The allosaurus was wrapped in a black plastic garbage bag. I set it on the floor between my legs. Mom strapped Millicent into her car seat. Jen crawled into the car next to Millicent.

Dad began his run-through. "Everyone went to the bathroom?"

"Yes," we all said.

"You unplugged your curling iron, Jen?"

She let out a sigh. "Yes."

"Seat belts, guys?" Dad asked.

By now we were antsy. "Yes!"

"Then we're off!" Dad pulled the SUV out of the driveway.

"No!" Millicent let out a howl.

Dad slammed on the brakes.

"What now?" he said.

"Lulu," Millicent cried, pointing to the yard. Lulu was chilling under a tree. Jen jumped out of the car, grabbed the elephant, and handed it to Millicent.

We started out of the driveway again and our headlights flashed on a sign nailed to a telephone pole.

Texas to L.A. is very far.

You'll spend hours in the car.

"Isn't that clever?" Mom said. "Someone left us a funny good-bye sign."

"Maybe it was Lulu," Dad said.

I knew better. Amberson *had* been spying on us these past few weeks. That stupid sign proved it. My only hope was that he didn't know anything about me trying out for *Mania.* If he did, I was doomed.

chapter
eleven

"Before long I'll be reaching into the box," Mom said enticingly, giving the small cardboard container on her lap a shake as we traveled down the highway.

Each of us had put three wishes in Mom's box for where we'd like to go. Mom planned to draw one a day when we got to California. Whatever she drew would be the place we'd see that day. Jen wanted to see Disneyland, the Los Angeles Ballet, and Rodeo Drive. I knew Mom would vote for Hollywood and a tour of movie stars' homes. And Dad was eager for all of us to see the Pacific Ocean. Freddy wanted to drive out to Long Beach and visit the *Queen Mary* in dry dock. Each of my wishes was the same: *Masquerade Mania!* I had three shots at my dream. Millicent didn't care what we did as long as she had Lulu with her. They'd go anywhere.

"Mom's gonna pick *Masquerade Mania* first. I just know it," I said.

"Mr. Pinkie, your chances of getting on that show are about as good as walking on the moon," Jen said.

"And what makes you think I can't do it?" I asked her.

"Because you have to be cle-ver." She flipped her hair. "Since you're just a twerp, I doubt they'd even know you were there."

"Ha!" I said, shifting my body. There was barely room for my legs with the allosaurus head at my feet but I didn't complain. "Just wait. When I get on the show and win a trip for four to Hawaii, I'll choose Freddy to go instead of you. You'll have to stay with Aunt Kate and Millicent." She made a face at me.

"Jen is right," Dad said from behind the wheel. "Trying to get on TV is a hard thing to do. I'm willing to let you take a chance, I just don't want to see you disappointed."

"And America doesn't want to see you on TV," Jen muttered.

I stuck my tongue out behind her back. She could be as negative as she wanted. It wouldn't stop me.

Dad whizzed down the highway, humming away like he was the happiest camper in the world.

"It would be nice if we had one of those little portable TVs in the car," I said.

"If you were watching TV all the time, you'd miss the scenery," Dad said.

Scenery? I sighed as I gazed out into the early-morning darkness.

Mom turned around and handed Jen, Freddy, and me each a bright-colored packet. "When it gets light outside, take a look. There are games, questions, and reading material about interesting things along the way. What you don't know you can look up in one of these," she said, passing back a canvas tote bag filled with reference books. "Whoever gets the most answers correct gets to put an extra suggestion in the box." The last part was good, but still, we all groaned.

"Mom, we just got out of school for the summer. This is supposed to be a vacation. Remember?" I let the packet drop on the floor by my dinosaur head and curled up on my side of the car to go to sleep. It was going to be a long day. Dad had said we would drive all the way to El Paso. That was six hundred miles! Texas was so big you could drive all day and not even get out of the state.

The sun came up and we could see the countryside. We passed Abilene, Sweetwater, Midland, Odessa, and Pecos. It seemed like El Paso was at the end of the world. I didn't think we'd ever get there. Every Texas town we drove through looked the same. Strip malls, gas stations, fast-food restaurants—reading all their names made me hungry.

"Hey," I said. "I'm starving. Can we drive through a Muffin Man and get something to eat?"

"You've had your breakfast," Dad said.

"That was a long time ago," I reminded him. "I'm a growing boy. Have you forgotten?"

Jen leaned over the backseat. She had a silly smile spread across her face.

"What?" I asked. "Don't you want something to eat? You've never passed up anything before."

"Remember how you used to think the voice in the microphone inside the Muffin Man was your special friend?" she said. "Mom would let you order your own kiddie meal? You liked ordering food so much you wouldn't eat Mom's food unless she'd let you yell in her face?"

Freddy started laughing.

I glared at her. "What's your point, Jen?" Other than to make me look like a dork, which was always her point.

"You'd drive your tricycle up to the table and Mom would say, 'May I take your order?' And you'd say, 'Hi, it's me, Jason. A kid's meal with no sauce, just plain meat and a bun, and a basket of hot muffins. Thank you very much.' "

Freddy was cracking up. I wanted to strangle him.

"We're going to have to go to a drive-through," Jen said loudly. "Jason is having muffin withdrawal."

"Mom!" I yelled. "Jen's making fun of me."

"Jen," Mom said, "don't start." I couldn't believe it.

Someone was taking *my* side for a change. When he saw a Muffin Man restaurant, Dad pulled off the highway. We got out of the car to stretch our legs. Jen held on to Millicent's hand and we walked around the parking lot. After we got back in the car, Dad started through the drive-through. An employee bounced out the door, stopping beside each car.

"Have a box of muffins on us," he said. "It's a promo for Muffin Man's newest muffin." He shoved the box through the window. The hot muffins smelled terrific.

"What kind are they?" I asked, reaching for the one on top.

"Ooey-Gooey-Chewy Chocolate Delight," he said, smacking his lips. He handed Dad a card. "We'd like your opinion of our new muffin. If you'd fill out this card and mail it in to our office we'd appreciate it. And," he added, handing Dad a certificate, "your next stop at a Muffin Man is on us."

Dad took the muffins and passed them around. Jen handed Millicent a pinch of one. She took a bite and hot chocolate frosting oozed down her face.

"Yummy," she said. "More." She gave Lulu a bite. "More."

Dad ordered hamburgers and sodas. Since Mom had taken up for me, I decided that after I had eaten I would study her packet. The car was silent after we got our food. Traveling made us hungry, I guess. After I finished my hamburger and soda, I grabbed another muffin. They were delicious.

What is the capital of Texas? I wrote *Austin* in the blank. *Where is the Alamo and what is the date on it?* I knew the Alamo was in San Antonio but I wasn't good with dates. I was about to ask Freddy when Jen poked me. "No cheating!" she whispered. "Look it up!"

"I wasn't!" I whispered back.

Name some of the men who fought at the Alamo. Mom's questions were getting harder. But I didn't feel like using her books to help me. That made it too much like school.

"This is good trivia, Mrs. Percy," Freddy said. "You may have hit on a question they'll use on the show." He was right. I hadn't thought of that.

"Yeah, Mom," I said. "You've helped out a lot."

Davy Crockett fought at the Alamo but I was stuck after that. Freddy's pen raced down his paper. At the rate he was going, he was going to finish first and get to put an extra wish in the box. It looked like we were all going to see the *Queen Mary.*

The state of Texas has had three men serve as presidents of the United States. Who were they?

I wrote George Bush and George W. Bush but I couldn't think of anyone else. I skipped down to the next question. In the blank next to *state flower,* I wrote *bluebonnet.* Everyone in Texas knows that!

We drove all day long. Mom told stories about when she was a little girl, like how she and her family took a trip across Minnesota. True pioneer times.

We pulled into El Paso about the time the sun was setting. "Pass your packets up to me in five minutes," Mom said. I had left some of my questions blank and I noticed Jen had done the same thing. "I'm going to check over them tonight," Mom said. The sky was streaked with orange. I noticed on the map Mom had put in our packets how close we were to Old Mexico. I forgot about the Minnesota landscape and stared out the window. El Paso looked different from the other cities we had driven through. The houses were adobe, and there weren't many trees in the yards. We passed a school and I saw lots of kids playing ball and racing on skateboards.

Mom checked her map to see where the campground was. It wasn't far off the highway. "Time," she called. We passed our packets up.

"At last," I said, stretching my arms. My hands brushed Jen's hair. She was too exhausted to protest.

After ten hours in the car, my eyes could barely focus. Freddy and I had practiced game show questions, worked on the packets, and played video games. Jen and Millicent had sung "The Itsy Bitsy Spider" until Freddy and I begged for mercy. And if I heard "The Three Bears" one more time, I was going to suggest they put Goldilocks in jail for breaking and entering.

Dad turned down a dirt road and we saw campers in the distance. Airstreams the size of Greyhound buses were parked all over the place. As we drove to the office a million eyes followed us. I knew what these people were thinking. *What's a nice sardine tin like that doing in a place like this?*

I scooted down in my seat so no one could see me. The manager of the campground came out to greet us. He held a silver-and-black bullhorn in his hand. He bellowed out his directions as he motioned for Dad to follow him. I was sure they could hear him across the border in Old Mexico. The other campers in the park hung out their doors and windows. Our Camp'otel was the entertainment for the evening as we followed the manager to our campsite.

The manager looked at his clipboard and checked off our name. "Slot number three-oh-three," he hollered. "Right this way!"

chapter
twelve

"Does that man need to use a bullhorn?" I asked. It was embarrassing enough being in the Camp'otel. "Everyone is looking at us," I hissed. "Drive faster, Dad."

"I can't run the poor guy over. I have no idea where our campsite is," he said. Freddy and I scooted farther down in our seats. "I have to follow him to slot three-oh-three. Just cool it, boys."

I peeked out the window. We had passed a couple of Airstreams. People were grilling steaks outside and kids swarmed everywhere. Mom waved at everyone as we passed. I knew what was spinning in her head. Mom is an organizer. She always coordinates the Fourth of July parade in our neighborhood, and she puts together a group of carolers at Christmastime. Dad pulled our SUV into the slot between two white RVs. The man with the bullhorn told Dad to come by the office to pay our deposit.

Dad hopped out of the car. "Will do," he said, thanking the man. "Just as soon as I put up our bedroom." Dad patted the sardine tin.

Mom crawled out of the car and introduced herself to the people in the next campsite. She would make friends with our temporary neighbors and before anyone knew what had hit them, she'd have the entire campground sitting around a fire roasting marshmallows.

Freddy and I started unloading the car. "I hope you remember the words to 'You Are My Sunshine' and 'The Eyes of Texas,' because I've got a feeling you'll be singing them tonight," I said. "Look over there." I pointed toward Mom. "I bet she's already signed people up for a sing-along." I opened the cooler and grabbed a couple of sodas.

"You're not serious, are you?" Freddy said. "I couldn't carry a tune in my jeans pockets. Don't you remember in Cub Scouts? Your mom always asked me to clean up when it came time for singing."

"I'm as serious as a broken leg. Wait and see."

The aroma of sizzling steaks floated through the air and my taste buds were working up an appetite for a good dinner. I didn't mention being hungry to Jen. I didn't want to hear the muffin story again.

"Mom," I begged when she came back to the car.

"Let's not invite anyone over tonight. Dad's tired from driving all day. Wait until tomorrow."

She smiled but she had that look of "you're going to love a good game of hide-and-seek with your new friends" in her eyes.

"Nonsense, Jason. A few camp songs and games will do us good. It's a great way to break the ice. Just a couple of choruses of 'Row, Row, Row Your Boat' and you'll be in the swing of camp life before you know it." She darted off. "I'll be back in a second," she said over her shoulder. "I just want to say hi to those people across the road."

Dad knew what to expect with Mom. He unlatched the sides of the camper, and when it popped up, a bedroom unfolded on top of our car like magic. Gasps sounded from RV to RV. I couldn't help feeling a little proud.

"Well, doesn't that beat all, Clyde," I heard the lady in the camper next to us say. "I never saw a contraption like that."

I wanted to tell her that we hadn't, either, until Uncle Dan and Aunt Kate had brought it to our house in the first place, but I decided if I kept quiet maybe everyone would forget about me. After I put up our tent, Freddy and I could sneak into it and stay out of sight.

The lady stood at the door of her trailer with a platter of fried chicken big enough to feed our family, too, but she turned and went inside without inviting us in. Clyde followed.

I could almost hear them crunching juicy chicken legs. My stomach growled.

"Jason," Dad called. "I need help. Bring me the ladder."

Freddy had walked over to check out the basketball court while I stayed back to finish helping Dad. "Can I set up our tent first?" I asked.

"Hurry up, then," Dad said. "We've got a lot to do to set up our camp before dinner."

I used a battery-powered pump to inflate our air mattresses. The tent was next. There was going to be plenty of room for Freddy, Dad, and me. Dad had decided to sleep in the tent after we invited Freddy to come with us. Jen, Mom, and Millicent would sleep in the Camp'otel. The tent was up in a matter of minutes. Dad handed me the Coleman lantern and a couple of flashlights.

"Jen's tired," I said. "She'll want to go to bed soon. Taking care of Millicent all day isn't easy." I felt a scowl cover my face. I realized it would be my turn tomorrow.

"Jen doesn't look tired to me," Dad said, raising an eyebrow. "Looks like she's already made a friend." I looked across the road and saw Jen talking to a tall boy about her age.

"Traitor," I muttered. Leave it to her to follow in Mom's mixing-and-mingling footsteps. Jen was becoming Miss Friendly number two. I ignored them. Millicent and

Lulu stood beside them. Poor Lulu was upside down with her trunk in the dirt.

I grabbed the box of muffins from the car. They were next to Dad's laptop. Freddy and I had already discussed it. If dinner didn't work out, there were plenty of snacks left. We weren't going to starve.

"Where's the ladder?" I asked. "I thought it was attached to the side of the camper."

"It is," Dad said, looking up on top of the car. He walked around the SUV and came back empty-handed.

"Well, so much for the ladder," he said, shoving his hands into his pockets. "I must have left it at home."

Mom was still visiting with our neighbors across the road. A few drops of rain began to fall, and she came back to the car.

"Put up the ladder and I'll make the beds," she said to Dad. She called for Jen and Millicent to come back to our camper. "It's going to rain. Get Freddy, too."

"There is one little problem here," Dad said sheepishly. "I forgot the ladder." I moved behind him in case Mom exploded.

"What!" she said. "How could you forget the ladder?" She gave him an exasperated look. But knowing Mom, she wasn't about to let the lack of a ladder defeat her.

Soon the little sprinkle had turned into a hard rain. Mom climbed onto the fender of our car and crawled across the hood. As she climbed up the windshield, she held the bed linens under her arm. The expression on her face said more than any words could have. She grabbed one of the windshield wipers for leverage but the wiper popped off in her hand. She threw it on the ground. The rain pounded harder. She started up the windshield again.

"I've done harder things than this," she called, her mouth set in a determined line. "I climbed the Himalayas when I was in college." Dad laughed. I didn't dare.

Freddy, Jen, and Millicent were back and witnessed the entire spectacle. The windshield was slippery and Mom slid down the hood several times. Her face was the color of strawberries by the time she managed to get inside the camper. Dad climbed onto the hood next and handed Millicent up to her.

"Rain!" Millicent said happily. By now the rain was coming down in sheets. We were all soaked.

"You and Freddy get in your tent!" Mom shouted down. "It looks like we're in for a real storm."

"Where's the ladder?" Jen yelled. Her voice was hard to hear over the downpour.

"I'm sure glad we set this up already," Freddy said as we dove into our tent. His red hair was standing up in wet clumps.

"The ladder!" Jen shrieked again, stomping her foot in the mud. "Where is it?"

I stuck my head out. "Ixnay on the adderlay," I said, relishing every glimpse of my wet sister. "Climb up on the hood and walk up the windshield just like Mom."

Jen's mascara ran in streaks down her face. She looked ready to kill somebody.

"It's a different way of camping," I said as she attempted to climb. "It's called 'too bad you aren't sleeping in our tent.'" Freddy and I doubled over with fiendish laughter.

Dad had jumped into our car to stay dry. Finally the rain stopped and he got out to attach the patio awning to the side of the car. It appeared he'd also forgotten to bring a hammer, however, so he pounded the awning stakes with the heel of his shoe. He pounded so hard that the heel flipped off and flew into the bucket of water he had collected for our dish washing. I wished I'd taken our video camera out of the back of the car but it was getting too dark to use it anyway. Too bad. It would have made a great blackmail film when I got to be a teenager.

Dad finished attaching the awning by using our iron skillet for a hammer. At least he had a dry place to cook. He was determined to make us dinner on our first night in the campground. I had to admire his persistence.

"Jason," he called. "Get me the stove. I'm going to cook us the best meal we've ever eaten." I crawled out of my nice dry spot and dragged the stove over to him. It felt slimy and wet and it was covered in mud.

"Do you think the rain's gone for good?" I said, looking at the black sky. It didn't look quite so angry anymore.

He turned his palm upward and shrugged. "Looks like the worst is over," he said. Then, as if we hadn't just been through the rainstorm of the century, he put on his apron. "Nothing like fried potatoes and bacon out on the open range," he said. "Just wait until you hear potatoes sizzling." He smacked his lips.

But instead of potatoes sizzling I heard rain falling. I dove back into the tent. I had to hand it to Dad. He was covered with rain and mud and he'd lost a shoe while putting his kitchen in place. His brown hair hung like wet strings in his eyes and his glasses kept sliding down his nose, but he was still trying to peel potatoes.

Mom stuck her head out of the camper. "Forget dinner, Pat," she called down to Dad. Her hair was bunched into soggy ringlets. "The only thing that should be out on the open range in weather like this is cattle. Before you drown," she said, "order pizza. We'll cook tomorrow night."

"The cell phone needs charging," Dad said. "Besides, we're out in the woods, Sarah. Pizza deliveries don't come out this far."

"Use the office phone," she said. "Tell them you'll give a tip. A big one!"

Dad folded up the lawn chairs and covered the

cooler and the rest of our camping gear with a big plastic tarp. Uncle Dan had told him to take one just in case we ran into rain. Ran into rain? We were in a Texas gully washer.

It rained so hard I thought we should be sleeping in our bathing suits. Freddy and I didn't want to read by flashlight and there was no TV. The rain pounded so hard that it was impossible for us to hear my portable radio. We went over trivia questions instead. Freddy was raring to go as usual.

"What's the highest peak in the continental U.S.?" he yelled.

"Mount Whitney," I yelled back.

"How long does it take to climb the Himalayas?"

"About as long as it took Mom to climb up our windshield," I said, laughing at my own joke.

"How long, Jason?"

"It takes three to four months from the northeastern side."

"Why would you need a whingo?" he said.

"Beats me. I don't know. Why would I need a whingo?"

If you played quidditch you'd need one," he said. "Better write that one down." He took a breath. "Which animal makes no sound?"

"The giraffe," I said, wondering why.

"How many notes are there in an octave?"

"Eight."

I looked out of our tent from time to time to check on things. Water gushed in the ditches beside the dirt road. A raging river appeared out of nowhere. We zipped up our sleeping bags and lay still on the air mattresses, listening to the downpour. After Dad had covered everything, he scrambled up the windshield and crawled into the camper to wait out the downpour with Mom and the girls. It took him five tries before he finally made it inside their little tent. He would join Freddy and me when he was ready to sleep.

Then the hailstones hit. The noise sounded like someone was outside our tent with machine guns. The *rat-a-tat-tat* was deafening. Hail pelted our tent. Our car. Our lawn chairs and every single bit of camping equipment we had unpacked. And when it got through with us, it started on the trees. There wasn't a leaf in sight. It moved to the RVs and beat on them as hard as it could. I looked outside. The ground was covered with hail the size of jelly beans. The wind blew so hard that if I'd been flying a kite, I would have been airborne. The hail stopped after about three minutes but the wind and rain continued. I was afraid it would blow the camper off our car and my parents would be lost forever, but the camper stayed intact. It was a real trouper.

Then, just as quickly as it had started, the storm stopped. The rain turned to a drizzle and it felt like a simple evening shower. That was what Texas weather did best. Kept you on your toes.

"Are you kids all right?" Dad called down to us. I poked my head through the tent flaps.

"Sure," I said back to him as droplets of water landed on my face. "What's a little pitter-patter?"

chapter
thirteen

"What a mess," Freddy said the next morning. The sky was as dark as a licorice stick.

I moved my flashlight across the ground. The red-and-white awning lay in a puddle of mud. Leaves were scattered everywhere. Lawn chairs were turned upside down and toys were blown across the road.

"Yeah. Maybe we can start by drying some of this stuff off," I said. I picked up the overturned camp stools and stacked them next to the car.

I flashed my light on Clyde's RV and couldn't help wondering if they had eaten all their fried chicken. I was starving. They had probably watched videos and eaten a nice dinner. "I bet if we had asked we could have seen *Masquerade Mania* on their TV."

"Too late now," Freddy said.

Our route today was going to take us into Las Cruces, New Mexico. Then sometime in the afternoon we'd be in Arizona. I let my flashlight take one more sweep around the park, surveying the damage. Across the way a boy was walking a golden retriever. I felt a pang. The RWU brochure had advertised a fax machine. There was a light on in the office. I still had on my jeans and I felt in my pocket for my money.

"I'll be back in a second," I told Freddy. "I'm going to send Carey Anne a fax about Patches."

"Tell her to leave my stuff alone," he said. "I set a trap for her. If she opens my door, *boom!* She's a dead duck."

"What kind of a dead duck?" I said.

"A wet dead duck," he said. "There are water balloons waiting for her if she opens my door."

"You've been around Amberson too long," I said.

I ran to the office barefoot so my shoes wouldn't get muddy. The man with the silver bullhorn sat in a chair behind his desk. His hair was sopping. Muddy boots sat by the door. His bare feet were propped up on the desk. He was watching a rerun of *I Love Lucy* and laughing like he was seeing it for the first time.

"Sir?" I said. "Can I use your fax?"

"It'll cost you two bucks," he said.

"I've got money."

He shoved a piece of paper at me and handed me a pen, then turned back to his program. It was the one where Lucy and Ethel climb over Jimmy Stewart's fence and the Japanese gardener calls the cops when he discovers them by the swimming pool. It was one of my favorite episodes. I watched it for a second and then I wrote a short message to Carey Anne. I asked the man for the number of the camp's fax so she could fax me back.

"I'm over in slot three-oh-three," I said, pointing in the direction of our camper.

"I know where you are," he said, not bothering to look at me. "Everyone in the campground knows where you are."

"If my friend faxes me back would you let me know?" I asked. "It's *important.*"

"Yeah, sure," he said absently, taking the paper and my money.

There wasn't much else I could do. I ran back to our camp. My feet were covered in mud and the bottoms of my jeans were wet. There were paper towels in the car and I grabbed some so I wouldn't get mud in my sleeping bag. I checked on my allosaurus head to be sure it hadn't gotten wet and then I crawled back into our tent.

Before long, I saw Jen climb down the windshield. Mom slid Millicent down to her.

"Hey, Mom," I said, "Freddy and I will help clean up

and we can be out of here before you know it." She looked like a soggy mess but she managed a smile. She wiped off the lawn chairs and picked up things that were scattered around the campsite. She was a real sport.

Dad trudged back from the bathhouse. "Aloha, folks. We'll eat at a Muffin Man restaurant on the highway since everything's still wet. But tonight I'll fix a real campers' dinner." Jen grabbed Millicent's hand and headed for the bathhouse.

"Don't be too long," I told her. "We're leaving as soon as possible." She gave me one of her looks.

"Hey," I said, "you forgot your orange shower cap." She stuck out her tongue and kept walking. It didn't take long to get things in order. Some of the people around us began to stir. Freddy and I dressed in our tent.

The man in the site next to us came out on his patio. "That was quite a storm we had last night, wasn't it?"

"I've seen worse," Dad said, picking up our camping gear.

"The missus and I were afraid you'd blow away in that camper of yours. How did you get along?"

"Couldn't have been better. This is our little miracle of miracles," Dad said, patting the side of the camper.

"Guess your car didn't fair too poorly," the man said, raising an eyebrow. "I was afraid with all that hail it would get ruined for sure."

Dad rubbed his hand over the hood of our SUV. There were hundreds of pockmarks on it. Poor Dad.

"Camping's always an adventure," Dad said with a nod. I knew he was sick about it but he didn't let on how he felt.

"Let's go," I said. "The sooner we're on our way the sooner we'll get to the Pacific Ocean."

"I'm with you, Jason," Dad said. "Here come the girls. We can get going." I jumped into the back. Freddy crawled in next to me and Jen got in on her side.

Just as we were pulling out of the campgrounds the man with the bullhorn came running out of his office. "Hey, kid," he called. His voice boomed out through his bullhorn. "You got an answer to your fax."

"Stop the car," I said as Dad rolled down the window. "What did it say?"

" 'Dear Mania Man,' " he boomed out. " 'Hope you have nice galoshes.' "

She didn't even mention Patches! Next time I'd send an e-mail and ask her to get something for me out of Freddy's room. *Boom!*

ⓢⓢⓢ

New Mexico looked different from Texas. Mom's packet said it was called the Land of Enchantment. Most of the countryside was dry and barren. There were adobe homes out in the fields and along the highway. We'd see children riding bikes and playing tag when we passed through a town. All kids seemed the same to me. They liked having a good time.

We had turned our Texas packets in to Mom when we arrived in El Paso. I wondered if she had read them by flashlight in the Texas storm. She had passed out our New Mexico packets as soon as we got on the highway. "All of you did well with Texas," she said. "I read them last night by flashlight."

I knew it! "But you need to look up New Mexico answers because some of the Texas answers were wrong."

"What was the date on the Alamo anyway?" Jen asked.

"You should have it looked up," I said haughtily. "You had to find out for yourself."

"*You* didn't," she said. "You skipped around. I saw you."

"Did not."

"Did too."

"Did not."

Mom leaned over the back of her seat. "Listen, you two," she said, "the one with the most correct answers gets to put an extra suggestion in the box. I think you should stop bickering and start reading." That was enough incentive for us.

New Mexico has the oldest road in the United States. What's it called? I was stumped. I put a red check mark next to that question.

Freddy's grandparents had a summer home in Red River, New Mexico. He'd been there tons of times. I went once with him but I got altitude sickness and I never wanted to go again. The altitude was 8,750 feet! It was too high for me.

When did New Mexico achieve statehood? I opened the book about New Mexico. I guess Freddy knew all the answers because he didn't ask to see the book once. Jen was looking at her ballet magazine. I bet she planned on peeking at my answers later. I covered my paper so she couldn't lean over the seat and take a look. That would serve her right.

"We just crossed the state line for Arizona," Dad said. "Who knows the biggest tourist attraction in this state?"

"The Grand Canyon!" we all yelled.

"It's too far north for us to see it," he added. I was disappointed. I wanted to see the Grand Canyon. "Not to worry," Dad said. "Our next camping trip we'll make it a point to go there." My stomach did two flips. Our next camping trip? No way was I gonna do this again. Freddy and I were already making plans to talk Dad into selling the Camp'otel to the kids who had bought our neighborhood newspaper. We'd cut them a good deal.

We pulled into the campground at the end of the day. At least I was more used to the stares now.

Freddy and I put up our tent while Jen and Mom set up the picnic table. Dad put up the awning. Millicent and Lulu sat contentedly on the camp stools and ate cookies. "One for you," Millicent said. "Three for me. One for you. Two for me." I kept my eye on her in case she decided to wander off and get lost. Jen was scanning the place for boys. I could tell by the way she was looking it all over.

The sun was setting and the sky looked orange and red. Not a cloud in sight. Dad started a fire. Mom left Dad to cook and started working her magic with the people who camped near us. I heard laughter from across the way and I knew she was entertaining them with some of her stories.

Freddy started to inflate his air mattress. "You lucked out last night," I said. "Mom's sing-along was a washout."

He grinned. "Yeah," he said. "I was thinking the same thing." He looked at his jeans. They were covered with mud from the night before. "We look like one big mud pie," he said.

As much as I hated to admit it, we were going to have to go into the public showers with total strangers and wash the mud from between our toes. "Guess we might as well get it over with," I said. "Showers, here we come."

We each had buckets where we kept our bathroom

stuff. I had intended to refuse to wear the goofy yellow flip-flops Mom had bought for me, but the threat of athlete's foot convinced me otherwise. Freddy and I piled our stuff together and headed for the showers. When we got to the building I heard earsplitting laughter.

"What's going on in there?" Freddy asked. I shrugged. Before we got the chance to go inside, Mom came flying around the corner of the building.

"Boys," she said. "I'm glad I caught the two of you. When you're finished with your showers bring all of your muddy clothes over to the Laundromat. If I can grab a spare machine I'm going to do wash tonight."

"But Mom! I'll have on my robe," I complained. "People don't wander around wearing robes and yellow flip-flops. There's a law against it. I read about it before we left home."

"Nonsense," she said. "Your muddy clothes are due at the Laundromat in ten minutes. No excuses." I looked around but Freddy had already gone inside. I ran back to our car and grabbed my allosaurus head. No one would know I was the kid from the silly camper.

The sign on the door of the men's showers said BUCKAROOS. I didn't know why people thought those signs were cute. I hated them. They put those same stupid signs in some of the Tex-Mex restaurants in Texas.

I put the allosaurus on my head and walked into the bathhouse. It was a perfect fit, and since there was no peanut butter inside it I knew I'd have no trouble getting it off. The Buckaroo shower was what I had expected: hot, steamy, and smelling like Lysol. I gagged. No one noticed me at first so I took a quick look at the strangers standing around. They were seasoned campers. They didn't act at all intimidated by standing around half naked with total strangers. I didn't see Freddy anywhere.

At the sink stood Mr. Neat and Tidy. He was trimming his mustache with a tiny pair of scissors. Over to the side stood Mr. I Don't Care. He reached into his mouth, yanked out a set of false teeth, and set them on the sink. "Can't forget my molars," he said to no one in particular.

Gross, I said to myself. On the wet concrete floor was Mr. Please Don't Let Me Get Fat. He was doing push-ups and he was huffing and puffing worse than the ladies I had seen in my grandmother's aerobics class the time I went with her.

A shower door opened and out came Mr. Friendly Cowboy. He wore red-and-white-striped boxers, stovepipe cowboy boots, and a white ten-gallon hat, and he had a towel wrapped around his neck. He looked my way. "Well, I'll be a dadburned polecat if it isn't Tyrannosaurus rex." Everyone looked at me. The cowboy tipped his hat.

Before he could say anything else I ducked into a shower stall. The latch was broken but the door closed tight. I put my flip-flops under the door so people would know my stall was occupied. Then I undressed. The wooden door had cracks in it and I kept a close watch out for any peeping Toms. Thankfully everyone seemed too busy showering, shaving, and laughing to be bothered with me. My dinosaur head came right off. I put it on the bench and stepped into the shower.

When the water came on it was ice cold! "I knew it!" I muttered. I made a mental note to share that juicy piece of information with Miss Ballerina of the World. I planned to write the RWU Campground Association a letter telling them that they advertised falsely in their brochures. I intended to sue. I had hopped in and out of the shower in record time when I heard a familiar voice.

"I'm looking for two twelve-year-old boys. It's my son and his friend."

I wrapped my robe around myself, put on my allosaurus head, and opened the shower door. I marched out in front of everyone as if it was a natural thing for a dinosaur to be in the men's bathhouse. Dad looked shocked. I could see his face through the mouth of the allosaurus head. He wasn't smiling. Freddy opened up his shower stall and came out, too. He gaped at me.

"What's that?" someone said as I walked toward the outside door. Dad and Freddy followed me.

"Don't bother about him," Mr. Friendly Cowboy said, "he's just a dinosaur who dropped by for a shower."

When I got outside I started running. It was hard to run fast in flip-flops and a dinosaur head but I managed. I didn't wait to hear what Dad had to say. Freddy was right behind me.

We raced to the Laundromat to find Mom. Two ladies screamed when they saw me but I didn't care. Millicent and Lulu were playing with a small boy. The Laundromat was worse than the men's showers. There was water all over the floors and one dryer squeaked like the wheels on the grocery carts at our supermarket.

"Jason, take that head off and go put it back in the car," Mom said, laughing. She sat on a table where people folded clean laundry. Our clothes were in a pile beside her. I threw my muddy clothes down. Freddy pitched his in the pile, too.

"Aren't you hot in here?" I said, feeling sweat running down my neck.

"I would be if I had that silly head on. Go take it off! I'll be back as soon as we have clean clothes."

The dryers put out so much heat that I felt like I was going to pass out. "Let's get out of here," I said to Freddy.

"Why are you wearing your costume, anyway?" he said. "You don't want to ruin it, do you? Have you forgotten? It's the only one you have."

"I didn't want anyone to recognize me," I told him. "I don't like people staring at our Camp'otel. I wanted to be in-conspicuous. I don't want them to know I belong to it."

"Well, that's one way of being inconspicuous all right," he said. "Wearing a dinosaur head to the men's shower. That'll fool them for sure." He laughed.

"C'mon," I said. "Let's get back to our camp before I get into any more trouble."

We made it back to camp and put my dinosaur head in the back of the SUV. Mom came back lugging our muddy clothes in her arms. Millicent and Lulu were with her.

"The washers are all taken," she said. "I'll have to do laundry early in the morning before we leave."

"Let's eat," Dad said. He and Jen had set the table. "I didn't cook any dinosaur food, Jason, but would you settle for fried potatoes and hot dogs?" I filled my plate.

"Smells good," I said. "Allosauruses eat anything." After dinner, Freddy and I dressed again so we could go to the basketball courts.

"Michael Jordan," Freddy yelled, pitching the ball to me. I dribbled the ball down the court and made a slam dunk. "Yes!" I yelled, catching the ball when it fell through the net. I jumped up and did it again.

"Chicago Bulls superstar," I said. "Everybody knows that one."

"Name two L.A. Lakers," he said.

"Not us," I said. I knew most of the players but playing basketball and thinking at the same time was hard. "Wait a minute," I said, stopping to gather my wits. I leaned over and rested my hands on my knees to catch my breath.

"No waiting," he said. "You're gonna have to be fast."

"Shaquille O'Neal," I said. Then my mind went blank. My hands felt sweaty. I couldn't call another name. I dribbled the ball in circles. "Shaquille O'Neal," I said again, wiping the sweat from my face.

"Kobe Bryant," he yelled. "Faster, Jase. C'mon, you gotta be faster."

"That's it," I said. "I'm done. My brain is asleep."

But Freddy wouldn't give up.

"Name five dinosaurs," he said when we had crawled into our tent.

I groaned. Then I thought about the great prizes I'd win on the game show and the possibility of getting a real girlfriend when I got home. I named dinosaurs as fast as I could. I even threw in some dinosaur characteristics.

"Saltasaurus, covered in thumbnail armor; psitta-cosaurus, with its strong beak; apatosaurus, which ate vegetation from the treetops; triceratops, with its three horns, and stegosaurus—huge body, small head."

"What about the camposaurus?" he said.

"Huh?" I said. Then I realized he was joking.

"I'll give you a hint about the oldest road in New Mexico," Freddy said.

"Shoot," I said. "Jen will be furious if I fill that question out."

"El Camino Real is the oldest highway in the U.S.," Freddy said, "and New Mexico reached statehood in 1912. Write those in your New Mexico packet tomorrow. You'll have a better chance of winning if you get most of the answers right."

"Thanks," I said. "How did you find out?"

"Easy. A camposaurus told me," he said. "I know something else, too."

"What?" I said.

"The Alamo was built in 1718 as a mission. Davy Crockett fought there. So did James Bowie. I put those answers in my Texas packet," he said.

"Well, I blew that," I said. "I left those questions blank. I looked in the books but I couldn't find the answers before Mom called in the packets."

"Hmmmm," Freddy said. "Maybe we should let the camposaurus be on the show instead of you."

"Maybe so," I said. I zipped up my sleeping bag and rolled over to go to sleep. No way was I going to let a camposaurus or anyone else keep me from getting to be a true Maniac.

chapter
fourteen

The next morning when I opened my eyes, Freddy was gone. He'd probably left to shoot baskets. Jen was gone, too. She was probably out looking for cute boys. I saw Mom lugging our dirty laundry across the road as I crawled out of our tent. Dad was brewing coffee. Sausage patties were sizzling on the grill. My stomach growled loud enough to wake up a bear.

"I'm going over to the office," I told Dad. "I'll be back to help with breakfast. I need to plug in your laptop and send Carey Anne an e-mail. Your battery is almost gone and I want to check on Patches."

"Go," he said. "I can handle breakfast."

I ran to the office. "I need to plug in my laptop," I said to the lady at the desk. "Is that okay?"

"Help yourself. We aim to please. But you don't have to use your computer. We have computers here for the use of our campers. You can send an e-mail from here."

"I want to use my computer but I need to use your port. Is that okay?"

"Okay by me," she said. "It'll be three dollars."

```
Carey Anne,
How is Patches???? Is he eating ok?
Are you walking him? Does he look de-
pressed?
Write back!!
Jason
P.S. If you see Amberson (that annoy-
ing kid that bugs Freddy and me) don't
tell him we're going to California and
don't mention that we're trying out
for Mania. I wore my allosaurus head
in the shower last night. It's a great
costume.
```

"Can I wait in your office until I get an answer?" I asked. "This is an emergency."

"Suit yourself," she said.

I picked up a dog-eared *Sports Illustrated* and flipped the pages. "Look at that," I said, pointing to a photo of a man standing on a mountain of dollar bills. "That guy must have won the lottery."

The lady looked over my shoulder at the magazine. "Yeah," she said, "I had a cousin who won some money once at the grocery store. He won fifty dollars and a dozen eggs. I've never won anything but some bug spray and it wasn't any good. The bugs love it." She went back to her desk.

"I've never won anything either," I said, "but I'm getting ready to win a trip to Hawaii, maybe."

She looked over the top of her glasses. "Really? How are you going to do that?"

"My family and I are on our way out to California and I'm going to try and be a contestant on *Masquerade Mania*. I have a great costume and I'm sure I can talk my way into getting on."

"I love that show," she said.

"I'm going as a dinosaur. I've never seen one on the show before. Have you?"

"We had a dinosaur in the men's showers last night," she said, laughing. Before she could put two and two together, Mr. Friendly Cowboy ran into the office.

"May Belle! May Belle!" he yelled. "Some kid slipped in the laundry room. All the washers are overflowing and bubbles are everywhere."

May Belle jumped up. "What happened?"

"Someone put too much soap in the washing

machines. Water's everywhere. The kids are going crazy. They're running and sliding through a million bubbles." May Belle rushed outside. I saw Mom and Jen running to our car. They grabbed the first-aid kit and started back to the Laundromat. I knew Mom could fix up the kid who had gotten hurt. I wasn't sure what Jen could do. I went back to our campsite without getting an answer from Carey Anne.

"What's going on?" Dad said, flipping a sausage patty.

I told him what Mr. Friendly Cowboy had said. "You know Mom. She'll fix the kid up and he'll be as good as new." I crawled up on the picnic table and let my feet dangle over the edge.

"We'll be in California later today and I'd like to get settled in our campground so we can do some sightseeing," Dad said. "I think we should have our first drawing tonight after dinner so we'll know where to head first. How about that?" I was so excited to hear the good news I could hardly believe it. *Masquerade Mania* was just around the corner. I could feel it in my bones. I planned to finish all Mom's questions before we crossed into California.

"Go tell Jen and Mom as soon as they're ready we need to eat breakfast and be out of here. Freddy is swinging Millicent. Get them, too."

I took off running. As I ran I passed the playground.

Jen was talking to some boy with blond hair. I *knew* she wouldn't be helping Mom.

"And," I heard her say as I ran by the swings, "I plan to do a lot of shopping on Rodeo Drive." She'd be lucky if she could afford a pair of socks there.

"Hey, Jen," I yelled. "Dad said come eat breakfast and pack up your gear."

She didn't turn around. "Jen!" I yelled. "Dad said we're leaving soon. Unless you want to stay here with your boyfriend."

"I'll be there in a minute," she said, scowling at me. She was careful not to be too nasty—she didn't want to reveal her true self.

We had finished eating our muffins and sausage when Mom got back to camp. She had our laundry in black garbage sacks. She set them on the table. Jen was with her. I saw the boy who had been hurt limping to his camper.

"Was it serious?" Dad asked.

"No, just a bad sprain. He'll be okay." She looked at our laundry and started laughing. "I've got good news and bad news."

"Uh-oh," I said. "Not again. What's the good news?"

"All our laundry is clean and we're ready for California!"

"What's the bad news?" Dad asked.

She looked at us and burst out laughing again. "All our underwear is bubble-gum pink."

I froze. "My underwear is pink?"

Mom patted Millicent's curly little head. "I don't know how or when but Millie put Lulu in the hot wash and she bled on everything."

Millicent grinned, holding up a faded Lulu for us to see. "See?" she said. "Lulu clean. Mud all gone."

"My underwear is pink, too, Mrs. Percy?" Freddy asked.

"I'm afraid so. All the underwear is pink. But no one will know. After all, underwear doesn't show."

Freddy and Jen thought it was hilarious. I was the only one who was horrified.

"What if we're in a wreck and the doctors and nurses see our underwear? What if there's an article printed about us in the paper and some journalist says we were all wearing pink underwear when we died on the highway?" I was furious. Millicent started crying.

"Jason, you're such a twerp," Jen said, picking Millicent up. "Just be glad you *have* underwear." An evil glint came into her eyes. "Besides, everyone knows you love wearing pink."

chapter
fifteen

Thanks to Mom's packets, we learned that the Grand Canyon is 277 miles long. The grizzly bear is California's state animal. The Sequoia National Forest redwoods are the oldest trees in the world. But all that paled compared to what we learned next.

"California is the Golden State!" Freddy and I shouted when we crossed the state line. We were finally here! I stared out the window hoping to see someone famous. But there were just billboards for fast-food places and lots of traffic. Not a movie star in sight. It was hard to imagine anyone camping in L.A., but Mom had done her research well and right next to Disneyland was an enormous campground. Of course, we'd be camping on cement, but I would have camped on a sack of nails by then.

After we settled into our camp spot in Anaheim, Dad took out the box. "Okay," he said. "All packets in? Right?"

Mom nodded. "I've checked each one. Everyone did a great job," she said. "Freddy had the most correct answers, so he's the one who gets an extra choice to put in the box." Freddy took a bow.

"Way to go," I said, hoping he'd put in the TV studio for me. Jen had a scowl on her face but no one paid attention to her. We were all too excited.

"Maybe Freddy chose the ballet," I whispered to her. She punched me in the back and walked away.

"Okay," Dad said. "Let's draw."

I crossed my fingers, then my toes, and closed my eyes. I was afraid to breathe. Mom drew the first sheet of paper.

"A tour of movie stars' homes!" she yelled out. I was sad and glad at the same time. She deserved it. Mom had planned the trip, bought the food, written the packets, and done everything she could to make us all comfortable. It was only right that she got to do what she wanted. I didn't want to be a spoiled brat so I acted excited, too. I had three chances to go to *Masquerade Mania*. It would definitely happen—just not tomorrow.

"Movie stars' homes it is," Dad said. "We'll catch a tour bus in the morning and see where the stars live."

"I can't wait to check out Hollywood," Jen said, tossing her hair. "Maybe I'll be discovered. You can tell people that you knew me back in the day."

"Sad, isn't she?" I whispered to Freddy.

ⓄⓄⓄ

The tour bus was packed. Freddy and I found a seat together near the front.

"Hello, hello," a young man said, bouncing onto the bus. "I'm Toby, your tour guide." Green-and-red sunglasses were perched on his head and his yellow sandals matched his sunshine yellow shorts. A million heavy gold chains hung around his neck along with a brass whistle. If we couldn't see him, at least we'd hear him.

"Welcome to Hollywood," he said into a tinny portable mike. "You're going to see fabulous homes." There was a tattoo of a surfer on his left arm that said RIDE THE WAVES.

Freddy nodded toward his gold chains. "If he rode the waves, he'd sink!" Toby looked weird, but he was so friendly I couldn't help liking him.

The bus headed out Sunset Boulevard. Jen kept her nose pressed to the window and so did Mom. We headed down Roxbury Drive. "On the left is where America's favorite redhead, Lucille Ball, lived. Next door to her, in that big brown house, was Jack Benny's home."

I didn't know who Jack Benny was, but all the grown-ups looked impressed.

"Didn't Lucy live in that apartment in New York?" Jen asked.

"That was just for the TV show!" I whispered back. Jen swatted me away like a mosquito.

The homes were the biggest I'd ever seen. They made Amberson's house look like a cottage. The mansions had manicured lawns and iron fences with PRIVATE! KEEP OUT! signs on them. The driver stopped the bus for us to get out for a better view. A man with five cameras jumped off first.

"This is a Kodak moment," Toby said. "We'll have a twenty-minute stop here. If you'd like to follow me, I'll point out the different homes in the neighborhood and tell you who lived there in Hollywood's heyday and who lives there now. Follow me."

"Wait a minute, Freddy," I said, holding his arm as the crowd surged forward. "I want to check this one out."

My parents and Jen were so entranced that they didn't even notice we weren't behind them.

I pointed to the house in question. It was brick, with a huge balcony. But the best part was the line of gargoyles perched along the rooftop. Nobody had gargoyles back in Texas.

I hopped up onto the low fence framing the yard.

"Are you crazy, Jason?" Freddy hissed, looking around in a panic. "You could—"

Before I knew what was happening an alarm sounded. Guard dogs appeared out of nowhere and a man came running to the fence shaking a rake at me. Big mistake. Big, big mistake.

"Hey!" the man yelled. I guessed he was the gardener. "What do you think you're doing? Get off that fence!"

Freddy ducked into some bushes.

I froze. "I didn't mean any harm," I told the gardener nervously as the dogs growled. "I'm on a tour bus and they let us off to take pictures. I climbed on this fence to get a closer look. I'm sorry." I saw a lady in a wheelchair sitting under an umbrella by a swimming pool. She called out to the gardener.

"What's the commotion?"

"Just a boy on the fence, Miss La Faye. He wanted to look at your house."

La Faye, La Faye. Could this be Josephine La Faye? She was in a ton of the old movies Freddy and I had. If it was her, she must be about a hundred years old by now.

"Bring him over," the lady said.

"Do those dogs bite?" I asked without moving. One of them crouched down and his mouth curled up in a snarl.

The man said something in a foreign language and the dogs sat down. The gardener motioned for me to follow him, and with one eye on the dogs, I walked slowly over to

Miss La Faye. The gardener ran to turn off the alarm. Freddy stayed out of sight.

"Just what did you think you were doing, young man?" She wore a crisp white shirt and pale blue pants. A wide-brimmed hat shielded her face from the sun. "Don't you know this is private property?"

"Yes," I said, trying not to stare. She had a face full of wrinkles but I recognized her as the actress from those old movies. "I'm on a tour of movie stars' homes."

"Pooh," she said. "Those tour buses are frauds. They don't know where anyone lives. They make up all that stuff and the tourists don't know the difference. You pay good money for a pack of lies."

She looked expectantly at me. I didn't know what to say.

"Your house is awesome," I blurted out. "I wish my friend Freddy could see it."

"Where is he? On the fence, too?"

"He's hiding in the bushes. He was afraid we were going to get in trouble." I swallowed. "You're not going to call the police, are you?"

Her eyes sparkled. "Not unless you do something heinous." Then she laughed. "The police don't like to come here. They're afraid of my dogs."

"So am I," I said, looking around for them.

"Pshaw. They're gentle as kittens." She smiled over at

me. "I don't get many visitors here so I'll make a deal with you."

"A deal?"

"Since you bought a ticket to see movie stars' homes you're going to see a movie star's home. Deal?"

"Wow!" I said.

"Go get the busload of people," she told me. "We're going to have an open house." She reached for a glass of her lemonade. "And grab your friend from the bushes!"

Miss La Faye couldn't have been nicer. Once Freddy and I were able to convince everyone in the tour group that we weren't kidding, she gave us a tour of her home. She even had an elevator so she could get upstairs without help. Then she let us sit by her pool and drink lemonade while she entertained us with stories about what Hollywood had been like back in the beginning. She had started out in the movies when she was fifteen and had been a star for over eighty years.

"This is just like *Cribs*!" Freddy said, high-fiving me.

When it was time to leave, Freddy and I were the last to go to the bus.

"I can't thank you enough, Miss La Faye. This has been the best afternoon of my life." I shook her gnarled hand. "Now if I can just get on *Masquerade Mania*, my trip to California will be a big success."

"I watch it every night," she said warmly. "That's what

life is all about. Having fun and laughing. I'll be looking for you boys."

"I'll be wearing a dinosaur head," I said. "An allosaurus."

"Sounds good to me. If I weren't in this chair I'd go with you. But when you're ninety-five you don't get to do many fun things."

When we got on the bus everyone cheered. It had been a fabulous day. Toby said it had been the most successful tour he had ever given. "You've got guts, kid," he said. He'd tried to get Miss La Faye to open her home up to every tour group but she wouldn't have any part of that.

Jen had her nose glued to the window again. "What did you think of Miss La Faye?" I asked her.

"Fabulous," she said. "But you could have been arrested, you know. You lucked out this time." Her face broke into a grin.

"What?" I said.

"Just thinking. That's all."

"Thinking what?"

"About what the police would have said when they frisked you for a weapon and saw you were wearing pink undies." She exploded in laughter.

When we got back to the camp, I used a phone port to open Dad's laptop. Carey Anne had sent an e-mail.

Hey, Mania Man,
Patches is fine but he still can't run
as fast as Bruno. Your uncle Dan can't
run at all. LOL
Carey Anne
P.S. I already told Amberson about you
getting on the show before you told me
not to mention it.☺

chapter
sixteen

Each day Mom drew a different piece of paper out of the box. We saw everything there was to see in southern California. We were the ultimate California tourists. When I got my first glimpse of the Pacific Ocean I almost stopped breathing. It was as fantastic as Dad had described. There was water as far as I could see. I squinted at a ship miles out into the ocean. It looked the size of the boats in Millicent's bathwater.

We rented chairs one day at the beach and spent the day building sand castles and playing volleyball with a bunch of kids. Our skin turned blue when we dove through the waves. Jen flirted with all the lifeguards. She dipped her toes in the water once, then said it was too cold for swimming. Mom and Dad lay in the sun, soaking up all those California rays. Millicent made sand pies and she and Lulu gave tea parties all day.

Disneyland was a blast. I liked the Electrical Parade at California Adventure. Freddy and Jen loved the rides. My heart skipped a million beats when we raced down the rails and did flips and turns so fast I couldn't think. They went too high and too fast for me. The Indiana Jones ride was cool, though. And it was fun taking Millicent on the teacups.

It was great to be able to watch the fireworks every night when the park closed. Everyone in the campground enjoyed them. Millicent clapped when Tinker Bell slid across the park on a high wire, throwing kisses and waving to the crowd. It was fabulous.

The day we visited Knott's Berry Farm we saw Britney Spears and Jen asked for her autograph. Freddy and I wanted it, too, but we were too embarrassed to ask. When we visited Rodeo Drive, Freddy thought he saw Will Smith but it turned out to be just a guy in a snazzy suit. Jen bought a T-shirt that said RODEO DIVA in blue glitter.

Pretty soon we had only one week left. I couldn't believe *Masquerade Mania* hadn't been chosen yet.

We were eating dinner in this great Mexican restaurant when Mom said what was on all our minds. "Our trip's almost over, guys. I think you'll all have to agree we've seen the best California has to offer." I felt a lump in the pit of my stomach.

"Our trip isn't over yet, is it?" I said. "We still have other things to do, right? Like the *Queen Mary*?" *And* Masquerade Mania*!* I wanted to shout. But I didn't want to give Jen the satisfaction. "Right?"

Everyone was grinning. "What?" I said. I couldn't stand it any longer. "What's going on?"

"Jase," Dad said. "You've been more than a good sport about this trip. You camped when you didn't want to have any part of it. You survived a Texas storm without complaining. You've helped set up every day. You haven't fussed about the food." He looked at Mom, grinning. "You're wearing pink underwear as we speak. And not once have you acted ugly when the game show wasn't drawn."

"But it couldn't have been drawn," Mom said.

"We planned it that way," Dad said.

I was stunned. "You mean I never had a chance?"

"We pulled the game show out of the box from the beginning."

I felt sick to my stomach. "You did *what*?" I yelled. I couldn't believe it. My own family had betrayed me. This was the kind of trick Ambie Boy would pull. My eyes filled with tears.

"Jason, you're not paying attention," Mom said. "Dad didn't say we never intended to let you try. We decided since it meant so much to you and Freddy, we'd save our last couple of days to give you lots of chances to get on the show. You may not make it the first try, so we thought we would give you extra days." Everyone laughed. I felt like a dope. I rubbed away the tears that were threatening to give Jen ammunition for the next century and started laughing, too.

"You mean it?" I asked. "I'm going to get a chance to be on *Masquerade Mania*?"

Jen actually looked happy for me. For once she didn't say anything mean.

"We have another surprise for you," Dad said. "Your class is going to watch *Mania* together this week, hoping to see you. They all know to look for you in that silly dinosaur head."

"The whole class?" I said. Wow! That meant Kara Kaye would see me on national TV. It also meant Ambie Boy would see me. That would show that copycat a thing or two!

⊚ ⊚ ⊚

The next morning I was too nervous to eat. I had dreamed about this day for so long that now that it was happening, I felt scared. I was dressed and ready to go before anyone else woke up. We had to be at the studio extremely early. They only let the first hundred people in line try out for the show.

"If we get through in time at the TV station we can take in a couple of museums," Dad said, consulting his AAA guidebook.

I would have agreed to anything. My day was finally here!

The traffic was unbelievable on the Los Angeles freeway. Dad made two wrong turns and we had to double back twice. Mom did the navigating and got us back on track in no time. She was a whiz with the map.

"Hurry!" I said, drumming my fingers on the seat. "We've gotta be there early." I looked at my watch. It was already six-thirty. We had to be at the studio by seven o'clock or it would be too late.

"It's about two more blocks," Mom said. "I think you turn left for the visitors' parking lot. I saw a sign back there."

"That's it!" I yelled. "Up ahead." I pointed to a large building.

People were already lining up. Some of them were in costumes. Others were standing around watching the crazy activities. Dad pulled into a parking spot. I ran around to the back of our car and grabbed my garbage sack. It felt light. When I looked inside I couldn't believe what I saw.

"Pink underwear?" I screamed. "Where is my allosaurus?" Mom and Dad looked at one another. Then Mom put her head in her hands.

"I cleaned out our car so we'd have more room. I took

out your dinosaur head and set it on the picnic table to re-arrange things. I must have left the allosaurus at the campground."

"My allosaurus is back at the campground!" I couldn't believe what she had just said. "How could you do that?" Freddy looked stunned, too.

Mom started crying. "I know how much this means to you, but... can't you go as yourself? Just a twelve-year-old boy who wants to be on a game show?"

I felt like crying, too. "No way!" I said. "I've got to have a costume or I won't have a chance."

"We'll think of something," Dad said, looking desperately around us. "Maybe Mom can make you a funny hat out of a paper sack or something. What about that?"

About that time Jen raced around to the back of our SUV. She started throwing things out into the parking lot.

"What are you doing?" Freddy asked.

"I'm looking for something," she said, not looking up. "I'm going to make Jason a costume."

"I'm not wearing your orange shower cap if that's what you're thinking," I snapped. "That's out. Forget it! I'm out of the running to get on the show." I stomped off across the parking lot.

"Come back here, Jason," Jen called. "I have a great idea." I turned around to see what she thought was so great. She held Mom's first-aid kit.

"You want me to go as a Band-Aid?" I said.

"Mr. Pinkie, you're going to have the best costume in all of California." She pointed to my legs. "Take off your jeans."

"No way," I said. "I'm *not* wearing underwear for a costume. Is your head full of marbles?"

"No one expects you to be on TV in your underwear, you twerp. I'm going to wrap you in gauze, and you can't be bulky. Now strip." It sounded crazy, but I didn't have a choice. I hid behind the car door and did as she said. Jen pulled out spools of white gauze and started wrapping me like a mummy. When Freddy realized what she was doing he pitched in and helped. Before I knew what had happened I was wrapped from the tip of my head down to my ankles. They cut eyeholes so I could see and a small hole for my nostrils so I could breathe. Then they cut a tiny circle for my mouth so I could speak.

"Don't wrap his legs too tight," Jen said. "He at least has to be able to take tiny baby steps." They wrapped my arms separately so I could push the buzzer if I got chosen to sit in the Hot Box. When they were done everyone clapped.

"You look fantastic," Freddy said, nodding.

"You really do," Mom said, wiping her eyes. "And I'm not just saying that."

Millicent looked frightened.

I gave her a small smile that she couldn't see.

I felt like I was on my way out of surgery. Jen guided me across the parking lot and we headed to the area where the producers came out to pick the contestants. I heard everyone yell and I saw a zillion crazy signs. The girl next to me was a mermaid. Freddy said she was wearing a terrific costume but because of her one tailfin she kept falling over on the ground. I saw a fireman, a policeman, and someone dressed as a pig.

I had remembered to stuff my jeans pockets with all the extra things Jasmine and Desmond O might ask to buy, but I couldn't worry about that now. All I could hope for was a chance to get on the show. Freddy stood beside me and told me about each costume as the people came into view.

"There's a robot next to you, too," he said. "Here comes a ghost, and I see at least two pirates," he whispered. "They look washed up," he said. "They'll never get picked."

Five producers came out and the people went wild. I couldn't yell very well since the hole for my mouth was small, so Jen stood behind me and yelled. I felt like a mummy dummy with my big sister as the ventriloquist.

"Choose me!" she screamed. "Look this way! Pleeeaaase!" One judge looked our way but he didn't stop.

"Everyone needs a mummy," Freddy hollered over and over. I never saw him act so wild. The judges picked the robot, a scarecrow, and two girls who were dressed as Siamese twins.

"If we had that man's bullhorn from the campground we could get their attention," I said.

"Just hang on," Freddy said. "We're not about to give up yet. You're getting on that show if it's the last thing I do."

"Hurry," I said. "Get them to choose me." I felt sweat running down my back. My hands were numb and my fingers were stiff. My nose itched but I couldn't scratch because the hole was too small. I wanted to sneeze.

"Be still," Jen ordered. "You're coming loose." She pulled the gauze tighter around my middle. All I needed was for my costume to unravel and my pink underwear to show.

"Start humming," she said. "A producer is coming your way."

"Hum?" I said. "What for?"

"So they'll notice you, twerp. You don't want to look dead, do you?" I started humming the theme song from the show. A producer walked past me. I hummed louder.

"Hey, kid. You with the water pitcher on your head," he said. "You're on. Step to the right and get in line with the other contestants."

I hummed louder.

"Okay," the producer said. "I'm convinced. Everyone needs a mummy. Cut out the humming and stand in line with the rest of those people over there."

"All right!" Freddy said, high-fiving me through the gauze.

Jen looked totally proud. "I rule!"

I took baby steps to get over to the other people who had been chosen and followed the producers into the studio.

My heart was pounding like crazy. No one back home would recognize me, but thanks to Jen, I was one terrific-looking mummy.

"Okay, folks, listen up," said one of the producers. "*Masquerade Mania* is viewed by thirty million people and we want lively and happy contestants. Got it?" He motioned us toward an elevator bank. "We're going up to the studio now. When you get there you'll find out exactly what to do and where to sit. Any questions?"

"Sir," I said, "could you tell me how I can get to sit in the front row?"

"Listen to that," he said. "There's always a wise guy in the crowd. Here's a mummy who wants to be in the front row. Move it, kid. You'll have to take your chances like everyone else. Follow that scarecrow and get on the elevator or we'll choose someone else." I hopped toward the scarecrow. I didn't want to blow it now.

Once I got inside the studio I saw technicians, cameras, lights, and cables, and people running around in circles. All of the TV people wore soft-soled shoes so that they could move fast and not make noise. They raced back and forth across the stage adjusting scenery and cameras and anything else that needed attention. The show's band played the theme song and people laughed and clapped. The contestants stood up, which was a lucky break for me. I couldn't sit down wrapped like a mummy.

Someone from the show asked me my name and where I was from, then slapped a name tag on my chest.

I felt the spirit of the show immediately. No wonder Freddy and I had such a good time when we watched it. Everyone in the studio was having the time of their life. I wasn't in the front row but it was okay. I was close enough to see everything that was happening. The kid with the pitcher of water stood next to me.

The studio filled up quickly. My family and Freddy were in the upper section, where the spectators sat. I turned around to take a look. That's when I saw them waving and cheering for me.

I reached out and poked the water-pitcher kid on the arm. "Watch that water," I said. "If you jump around too much it's going to fall on me, and I can't afford to get wet."

"Just be glad I'm not balancing hot fudge sauce on my head. Then you'd have something to be concerned about," he retorted.

I guess he was right, but I still planned on watching that water. A wet mummy costume spelled T-R-O-U-B-L-E.

chapter
seventeen

When I looked down at the stage a man held five fingers in front of the camera. "Five, four, three, two, one," he said. "Let 'em roll." The *Masquerade Mania* theme song swelled up from the orchestra pit. This was it! We were on the air! Chills ran down my spine. Confetti and balloons floated from the ceiling. The audience went nuts and I started hiccupping like crazy.

Jasmine floated down the winding staircase. She was more beautiful in person than she was on TV. Her smile was awesome.

Desmond O dropped from the ceiling in a gold cage. "It's *Masquerade Mania* time!" he yelled. "Who wants to be a winner?" His bow tie blinked red and blue when he spoke. Everyone tried to get his attention.

"Want to win a prize?" Desmond asked a girl about Jen's age dressed as a cowgirl in a big hat and bolero vest.

"Yes, yes!" she cried.

"I'll buy your boots," Desmond O said. "I'll give you seven hundred dollars for them." The girl pulled her boots off and pitched them to him.

"Wait," he said, "you can take the seven hundred or you can exchange them for a look in this box." He held up a brightly colored box with a large red bow on top.

She hesitated. "Okay," she said. "I'll take the box." She shoved the money back at Desmond O.

When she looked inside the box you could have heard her scream all the way to Pasadena.

"Whoa!" she screamed, jumping up and down. She threw her hat in the air. "I can't believe it." She held up a pair of keys for the audience to see. I looked on the stage and saw a bright red Beetle. To the side of the stage a man held up an APPLAUSE sign and everyone clapped for her.

Next Jasmine asked a boy for a fishhook. He didn't have one but he sold his green handkerchief for four hundred dollars. Jasmine and Desmond O whizzed up and down the aisles faster than a pair of roadrunners.

"Where is the Grand Canyon?" Jasmine asked a boy. He looked about my age.

"California!" he yelled. Before he could correct himself, Desmond O shot the boy in the face with a water gun. It was filled with red water, probably raspberry soda. Everyone screamed with laughter. The boy laughed hardest of all. The show moved so quickly that no one had time to think straight.

Desmond O bought thimbles and zippers, and when he asked for a harmonica, I felt miserable. Millicent's harmonica was back in the car. "A thousand dollars for a harmonica," Desmond O screamed to the audience. No one had one. I didn't have time to be sick about it because Desmond O stopped by me next.

"Well, well, well," he said, reading my name tag. "I do believe we have a mummy from Texas." My hiccups grew stronger. "We have a mummy from Texas who has the hiccups." The audience burst out laughing. Desmond O held the microphone to my mouth and my hiccups echoed all over the studio.

"I know about mummies," he said. "They are *dead serious* about winning prizes. Don't you agree?"

"Yeah," I said. "I guess so." I didn't know what he wanted me to say. He laughed at his own joke. A siren went off backstage. I jumped a mile high. I wasn't expecting it. Desmond O's bow tie blinked as he talked.

"How would you like to sit in our Hot Box?" Jasmine said. I was so excited that I came close to throwing up right on national TV.

"No," I said. "I mean yes!" Jasmine guided me to the

Hot Box. I couldn't take my eyes off her. Her ginger brown hair reached below her waist and she smelled like Mom did when she went to a fancy party. Desmond O stopped in front of a guy and said something to him. He wore a reindeer head for a costume. The antlers must have reached out three and a half feet. I couldn't hear what Desmond O said to him but the next thing I knew, he pushed him into the other Hot Box to be my opponent.

Jasmine explained the rules of the game. "I'll ask the questions. First one to push the buzzer and answer three questions correctly gets a chance to Spin to Win. If you land on a square with a prize you may keep it, but if you land on a *WHOOPS!* you're in big trouble. Three *WHOOPS!* and you're out of the game.

"Okay," she said, smiling at us. She backed away from the reindeer so his antlers wouldn't poke out her eyes. "Are you ready?"

We both yelled, "Ready!"

"Name two of the six longest rivers in the world!" I slammed my hand down on the buzzer. I was glad Freddy and Jen had wrapped my arms separately because I wouldn't have been able to move them if they had attached them to my body.

"Nile and Amazon!"

"Good answers," Jasmine said, smiling. "One point for the mummy."

"Who were the main characters in *The Wizard of Oz?*" she said.

I slammed the buzzer again. "The Tin Man, the Lion, and the Scarecrow. And Dorothy," I said, for good measure.

"Good answers," Jasmine said again.

"Name the fastest mammal on earth."

Before either of us could answer, Desmond skated across the stage throwing marshmallows at us. "I'm the fastest. I'm the fastest," he cried. I wasn't expecting him to do that. By the time I regained my composure it was too late. I had looked at Desmond O and had lost my concentration for a second.

The reindeer's buzzer rang out loud and clear.

"The cheetah," he said.

"Good answer," Jasmine said. "One point for the reindeer."

"What did Harry Potter discover about himself?"

"He was a wizard!" we both yelled.

"You forgot your buzzers," Jasmine said. "Answers disqualified."

"Where do the Red Sox play?"

"Fenway Park," I said, slapping the buzzer. Desmond O ran across the stage throwing baseballs at us. One hit me in the nose but it was soft and didn't hurt. When it hit, it burst open and red gooey ooze dribbled down my chest. He hit the reindeer's head and knocked part of one antler to the floor. The audience clapped like crazy.

"Three answers correct! The mummy gets a chance to Spin to Win," Jasmine said. I took baby steps up to the board and gave the arrow a spin. Desmond O raced behind me on a skateboard. He skated so close to my backside that I wobbled off balance and I didn't give the arrow a good enough push. My first spin landed on a *WHOOPS!* When I turned around to see what to do next, he threw a pie in my face. I wiped the whipped cream off my eyes and licked my lips.

"Back to the Hot Box," Desmond O said, twinkling like a Christmas tree. The questions started to come faster. I couldn't catch my breath before Jasmine asked another one.

"What team has won the most World Series titles?" she said.

I hit the buzzer like wildfire. "New York Yankees!" I screamed.

"Next question," Jasmine said. "What's the capital of Rhode Island?"

"Providence," I said, pushing the buzzer as hard as I could.

"Two points for the mummy. Name the Great Lakes," Jasmine said.

Before I had a chance, the reindeer buzzed and called out, "Erie, Huron, Michigan, Ontario, and Superior."

"One point for the reindeer," Desmond said. "Lakes have lots of water." He skated across the stage and pitched a bucket of water in the reindeer's face. He came after me next and before I could duck, water splashed all over me. I looked down and I saw my skin through the gauze. I didn't dare move. What if my pink underwear showed?

"Next question," Jasmine said. "Name the seven continents." I gulped. I could never remember them all.

I slammed the buzzer anyway. "Africa, Antarctica, Asia, Australia, Europe, and...North America, and South America."

Jasmine smiled at me again. "Another Spin to Win for the mummy!"

I gave the arrow a giant push and it landed on a *WHOOPS!* Again. Desmond O grabbed me by the nape of the neck. I was ready for anything. "Time for the mummy dance," he said. I heard the clock ticking. He played his kazoo and I had to do a mummy dance all the way back to the Hot Box. I tried to remember some of Jen's weird dance steps but I couldn't move fast enough to do them so I just made up my own mummy dance. People clapped to the beat of the kazoo. I jiggled and wiggled like I thought a mummy might do if he'd taken dance lessons. The audience laughed so hard I could feel the building shake.

One more *WHOOPS!* and *zap,* I'd be out of the game. My nerves started to crumble.

Jasmine walked up to the mike again. "Name the four great oceans." The reindeer buzzed quicker than me.

"The Pacific, Atlantic, Indian, and Arctic!" he yelled.

Desmond O came onstage riding a unicycle. "You like water, don't you?" he said to the reindeer. A waterfall dropped from the ceiling and landed on the reindeer's head. To my surprise colored cooked spaghetti dropped next. Limp spaghetti hung from every branch on the reindeer's antlers. He was a mess. I looked down at my mummy body. So was I.

"Name five baseball players who belong to the five hundred club."

The reindeer was quick. "Mickey Mantle, Willie Mays, Ted Williams, Hank Aaron, Reggie Jackson." I could have named a zillion more.

"Spin to Win!" Jasmine told the reindeer. He ran to the spin board and gave the arrow a hard push. *WHOOPS!* Lights blinked throughout the studio.

"Come with me, Mr. Reindeer," Desmond said, beating a kettledrum across the stage. "Let's go sliding. If you can beat the clock you won't have to slide." He shoved the reindeer up a ladder and the clock began to tick loudly. In about a second, a bell rang. "Whoops!" Des said. "You lose." The next thing I knew, the reindeer was sitting in a tub of green Jell-O. He dripped back to his spot in the Hot Box. Jasmine stepped up to the mike again.

"Name the city where the Rose Bowl is played."

"Pasadena," I said.

"Name the state bird of New Mexico."

"Roadrunner," I hollered. Mom's packets had come in handy.

"Michael Jordan plays what sport?" Jasmine asked.

"Basketball," the reindeer screamed.

"Name the three Texas presidents," Jasmine said.

The reindeer slammed the buzzer. "George Bush, George W. Bush..." He stopped for a second. I heard the clock ticking against him again. I couldn't remember the last one, either. "Lyndon Johnson," he finally said just before the clock's bell sounded.

Jasmine smiled. "We are tied up and almost out of time. The next question will give one of you a Spin to Win if it's answered correctly. Just this week, the Muffin Man fast-food restaurants came out with a new muffin." Her eyes narrowed. "Name that muffin."

I couldn't believe my ears. My hands trembled. I slammed the buzzer so hard my whole arm throbbed. "Ooey-Gooey-Chewy Chocolate Delight!" I screamed. If we hadn't driven out to California I would never have known the answer. I scooted over to the spin board. My hands were still shaking and I had a knot in my stomach. I couldn't afford another *WHOOPS!* The audience began to chant. "Go, Mummy! Go, Mummy!" I could hear Freddy yelling louder than anyone.

I reached up for the arrow but I couldn't get a good grasp on it. My costume was unraveling and I tried to hold it so I wouldn't lose it. Some of the gauze on my fingers had come unwound. If I wasn't careful, I'd be responsible for the most embarrassing moment in the history of the show.

The noise was deafening as I reached up again for the arrow. I gave it the biggest pull I could manage. The arrow went around three times and landed on a trip to Hawaii plus a bonus spin! Sirens went off and soap bubbles floated from the ceiling. "Spin again," Jasmine said, "you've won a bonus spin!" I spun again with all my might. This time the arrow landed on free movie tickets for a whole year! Confetti and balloons dropped from the ceiling. The band played the show's theme song. Sirens blasted all over the studio and lights flashed off and on across the stage. The game was over and I had won!

Desmond O ran over to shake my hand. I reached out and grabbed it. He held a rubber snake in my face. I jumped back. MADE YOU LOOK, MADE YOU LOOK, MADE YOU LOOK, his hat said, flickering in red and blue lights. I was in a daze. Jasmine ushered me back to my seat. The kid standing next to me was laughing so hard that the pitcher of water fell off his head and water spilled all over me. I didn't even care. I was going to Hawaii! And I was now a true Maniac.

My family and Freddy ran up on the stage. "We did

it!" Freddy yelled. "We really did it!" Jen and Millicent were jumping up and down.

"You're the best manager in the whole world," I said. "I could have never done it without your help." I gave him a low five and a high five. I looked at Jen and my parents. "Or yours." I gave Dad and Jen a thumbs-up and Mom a huge mummy hug. "Thanks, Jen."

"That's okay, twerp, you deserved it," she said. "You did great, even if your pink undies do show." She reached over and snapped my waistband.

"We have to go backstage and sign for my prizes," I said. "That reindeer guy was good. Did you hear him? I almost didn't win." I looked over at the reindeer. He took off his head. One of the antlers had fallen off completely. He was grinning. What I saw startled me so much I came close to fainting. Neon braces!

"Amberson Anderson!" I cried. "How did you get here?"

"My grandfather and I were flying to Disneyland and thought it would be fun to see you in person. When we got to the studio, this kid in line got cold feet and backed out. He shoved this reindeer head at me and said I could have it. The rest is history."

His grandfather walked up and shook my hand. "Good job," he said. "You were quick with those answers."

"Thanks," I said, wondering if he liked to play tricks on people, too.

"Have fun," Mom said as they headed out of the studio.

"Hey, Amberson," I called. "You'll love the roller coasters at Disneyland. They aren't scary. I rode all of them." I tried to keep a smirk off my face when I told him that.

I didn't care anymore if Amberson was a copycat. Getting on the show had been *my* idea. I had done what Ms. Ware had taught us to do all year long. *If you don't follow your own dream, you will follow someone else's.* That dream would never belong to Ambie. It would always be mine.

"What are you going to do with your allosaurus head?" Freddy asked.

"I'm going to give it to Ambie Boy for his birthday. He wanted to copy so much, he can have it."

When we got back to the camp I checked my e-mail. I was in for another surprise. There was a message from Kara Kaye Barton! I opened it but I didn't dare read it out loud. Jen would never quit teasing me.

Dear Jason,
Congratulations! Our class saw you. We recognized your hiccups. Maybe we can go to the movies sometime this summer.

```
Your friend,
Kara Kaye
```

"Wow!" I might have a girlfriend in seventh grade after all. It had been the most exciting day of my life.

"Hey," Freddy said. "I want to ask you something. What does the *P* stand for in your name anyway?"

"Persevere," I said, grinning. "I put the *P* in my name myself. If you persevere, you can do anything. Ms. Ware told me that the first day of the school year. And I believed it." Mom and Dad were proud of me. So was Jen. Millicent didn't understand what had happened. All she cared about was the balloons bobbing around on the stage floor.

"Looks like we're making a trip to Hawaii," Dad said. "What do you think about that, Jason?"

"I can't wait!" One thing was for sure. We'd definitely have to fly. The Camp'otel had been pretty fun. But it was time to say good-bye.

chapter
eighteen

Freddy and I sat on the Hawaiian beach in front of our hotel soaking up the sun. I wiggled my toes in the sand. "Too bad Jen was already signed up for ballet camp," I said. "She could have been doing the hula with that lifeguard over there as we speak."

"This rocks," Freddy said, peering over the rims of his mirrored sunglasses. "Did I ever tell you, Jase, that you were awesome on *Mania*?"

"About a hundred times," I said, "but tell me again. It still seems like a dream." I rubbed more suntan lotion on my arms. "It's still hard to believe that I did it and won. Just think. We can go to the movies every day when we get home."

"I'll go anytime," Freddy said. "That is, when you're

not taking Kara Kaye Barton." I felt my face turn red, and it wasn't from the tropical sun.

"Hey. I have this fantastic idea," I said.

Freddy groaned. "Not again."

"Let's get a couple of Shirley Temples and an order of nachos," I said. "We can just charge them to the room like my parents do." I raised my hand and motioned for the beach waiter.

Mom and Dad were sleeping under a beach umbrella not too far away. With Millicent back with Aunt Kate, this was a true vacation. I guess Mom didn't want to organize an ocean sing-along. The competition—the gorgeous blue ocean to play in, volleyball courts, kids with shovels and pails building sand castles, and the surfers—would have been fierce.

The waiter came over. "What can I get you guys?"

"Two Shirley Temples with lots of ice and a million cherries, and loaded nachos," I said, flashing a smile. The waiter scurried off.

"Is this living or is this living?" Freddy said when the waiter came back with a tray.

"Just charge it to room sixteen twelve, please," I said.

"No need. It's already been taken care of," the waiter said.

"What?" I said, sitting up. "Who paid for it?"

"Those two gentlemen over there." I squinted to see if I recognized anyone. All I could see were about a million kids, and people sunning on towels and asleep in beach chairs. Not a familiar face in the crowd. Then I saw it.

"No!" I said, slapping my forehead.

Freddy snapped to attention. "What?"

"Look," I said, pointing to a striped beach chair. "Is that what I think it is?"

"You guessed it," Freddy said. "Antlers!"

About the Author

As a game show contestant, Diane Roberts won sixty pairs of shoes and a bright red coat. More rewarding is her career as a puppeteer, during which she has performed in front of thousands of children across the country, most often in the great state of Texas. Diane and her husband, Jim, live in Fort Worth and are the parents of three grown children. They have six grandsons. This is her first novel.